THE *list* OF THINGS THAT WILL *not* CHANGE

THE *list* OF THINGS THAT WILL *not* CHANGE

REBECCA STEAD

ANDERSEN PRESS

This edition first published in 2021 by
Andersen Press Limited
20 Vauxhall Bridge Road, London, SW1V 2SA, UK
Vijverlaan 48, 3062 HL Rotterdam, Nederland
www.andersenpress.co.uk

First published in hardback by Andersen Press Limited in 2020.

2 4 6 8 10 9 7 5 3 1

First published in 2020 in the United States of America by Wendy Lamb
Books, an imprint of Random House Children's Books, a division of
Penguin Random House LLC, New York.

'You Are My Sunshine' by Jimmie Davis copyright © 1940 by Peer
International Corporation. Used by Permission.

British Library Cataloguing in Publication Data available.

ISBN 978 1 83913 045 8

This book is printed on FSC accredited paper
from responsible sources

Printed and bound in Great Britain
by Clays Ltd, Elcograf S.p.A.

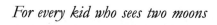

For every kid who sees two moons

The Sound of Corn

Just last weekend, my dad told me a story that explained one or two things about his wedding day. Not his first wedding day, the second one. The story was about him and Uncle Frank, when they were little.

They grew up in Minnesota, across from a cornfield where, every summer, the corn grew very quickly. Dad says the corn had no choice, because summers are short in Minnesota. It was either grow fast or don't bother.

Every year, Dad and Uncle Frank would stand together in the corn, listening to it grow. No one ever believed them, but they could hear the leaves squeaking, stretching for sun. They both heard the corn growing, Dad said, and no one else did.

"You never told me that before," I said. I liked thinking of them standing in the corn like that.

"I didn't?" Dad was flipping pancakes. We have this new

pancake griddle that covers two stove burners, so now he can make four at once. It's great.

"Did you hold hands?"

"Who?"

"You and Uncle Frank. In the corn. So you wouldn't lose each other."

Dad snorted. "No. Have you ever seen Uncle Frank holding hands with anyone?"

You'd probably never guess they're brothers. Uncle Frank is reddish-white, and my dad has a ton of brown freckles that give him a year-round face tan. Dad is a talker, and Uncle Frank . . . isn't. Dad loves food, every kind of it, and Uncle Frank says if he could live on one hard-boiled egg a day, he would be happy.

If you want to know what the sound of corn growing explains about my dad's second wedding day, I'll have to tell a longer story, about a lot of things that happened two years ago, when I was ten.

It's a story about me, but a *different* me, a person who doesn't exist anymore.

I have seen Uncle Frank holding hands with someone exactly one time that I can remember.

Angelica

The summer I turned ten, my cousin Angelica fell from the sleeping loft at our family's lake cabin. Uncle Frank says her head missed the woodstove by four inches.

She hit the floor with a bad sound, a *whump*. Then we didn't hear anything. No crying. No yelling. Nothing.

Until, finally, there was the sound of Angelica trying to breathe.

Dad got to her first. Aunt Ess, Angelica's mom, called from her room. "What was that? Dan? What *was* that?"

He answered, "It's Angelica—she fell, but she's okay. She got the wind knocked out of her, but I think she's okay."

From the loft, I saw Angelica sit up, slowly. Dad was rubbing her back in circles. Uncle Frank and Aunt Ess came crashing in from their bedroom, and then Angelica started crying these short, jagged cries.

The next morning, Uncle Frank said that if her head had

hit the woodstove, Angelica could have died. By that time, she looked normal. She was wearing her turquoise two-piece bathing suit and chewing her eggs with her lips sealed tight. No bruises, even—she landed on her back, Dad said, which is what knocked her wind out.

That summer, my parents had been divorced for two years already, but I still thought about when Mom used to come to the lake cabin with us. I could picture her red bathing suit on the clothesline. I remembered which end of the table she sat at for dinner. I remembered her, sitting on the dock with Aunt Ess, talking.

Mom and Dad told me about the divorce at a "family meeting." I had just turned eight. We'd never had a family meeting before. I sat on the couch, between them. They didn't look happy, and I suddenly got worried that something was wrong with our cat, Red. That they were going to tell me he was dying. A boy in my class that year had a cat who died. But that wasn't it.

Dad put his arm around me and said that some big things were going to change. Mom squeezed my hand. Then Dad said they were getting divorced. Soon he was going to move out of our apartment, into a different one.

I said, "But I'm staying here, right?" I looked at Mom.

Dad said I was going to have *two* homes, and *two* rooms, instead of one. I was going to live in both places.

I could think of only one person in my class whose parents were divorced: Carolyn Shattuck. Carolyn had a navy-blue sweatshirt with one big pocket in front. Until the family meeting, I had wanted one just like it.

I said, "What about Red?"

Mom said Red would be staying with her. "With *us*—you and me."

You and me. That made me feel awful. Because back then I couldn't think of Mom and me without Dad.

Dad said, "Things are changing, Bea. But there's still a lot you can count on. Okay? Things that won't *ever* change."

This was when they gave me the green spiral notebook and the green pen. (My favorite color is green.) In the notebook, they had made a list. The list was called Things That Will Not Change.

I started reading:

1. Mom loves you more than anything, always.
2. Dad loves you more than anything, always.

I skipped to the end, uncapped the green pen, and wrote:

7. Red will stay with me and Mom.

I said, "I want my rainbow to stay here, too. Over my bed." Dad painted that rainbow, right on the wall, when I was really little.

Mom said, "Yes, of course, sweetie. Your rainbow will stay right where it is."

I wrote that down, too. Number 8.

Dad moved into a different apartment a month later.

I go back and forth between them.

Here's how it works:

> MONDAY is a DAD day.
> TUESDAY is a MOM day.
> WEDNESDAY is a DAD day.
> THURSDAY is a MOM day.
> FRIDAY is part of THE WEEKEND.
> THE WEEKEND is FRIDAY and SATURDAY.
> THE WEEKEND alternates.
> SUNDAY is SUNDAY.
> SUNDAY is its OWN DAY.
> SUNDAY alternates.

Before Dad moved out, I thought of the weekend as Saturday and Sunday. Now I think of the weekend as Friday and Saturday. And I think of Sunday as SUNDAY.

Right after the family meeting, I found Red asleep in the laundry basket and carried him to my room, where I opened my new notebook. I looked at the list of Things That Will Not Change.

My parents had written:

> 1. Mom loves you more than anything, always.
> 2. Dad loves you more than anything, always.

6

3. Mom and Dad love each other, but in a different way.
4. You will always have a home with each of us.
5. Your homes will never be far apart.
6. We are still a family, but in a different way.

After that, I carried the green spiral notebook everywhere. I asked a lot of questions. I used the green pen.

Our first summer at the lake cabin without Mom, there were Mom-shaped reminders everywhere, like her blue Sorry! pieces and the chipped yellow bowl she always used for tomato salad. The Mom–reminders were all over the place, but I was the only one who saw them.

That summer, Dad explained to everyone at the cabin— Uncle Frank and Aunt Ess, and my cousins, James, Angelica, and Jojo—that he is gay. I already knew. My parents had told me at the one and only family meeting, when they gave me the notebook.

"Will you be gay forever now?" I asked Dad at the meeting.

Yes, he told me. He would always be attracted to some men the same way that some men were attracted to some women. It's the way he's felt since he was little. I uncapped my green pen and wrote it down right away on the list of Things That Will Not Change. It's number nine: *Dad is gay.*

After Dad explained about being gay to everyone at the lake cabin, he asked if anyone had questions. No one did. Then Dad and Uncle Frank walked down to the dock and sat with their feet in the water. I watched from the porch, where I was sitting on the edge of Uncle Frank's favorite chair. After a while, they stood up and jumped in the lake. They were splashing each other like little kids, laughing. I remember being surprised, because Uncle Frank never swims. He always says the water in that lake is too cold. Most of the time, he just sits on the porch, in his chair, in the sun.

"So, you live with your mom now?" my cousin James asked me that night in the sleeping loft. James is four years older than I am. I was eight that first summer without Mom, so he was twelve.

I explained to him about the days of the week. When I was done, we got into our beds, and Angelica tickled my arm for a while. (Usually, I tickled her arm, and then she would say she was too tired to do mine.)

Right around then, James started calling me "Ping-Pong."

He had really weird nicknames for his little sisters—he called Angelica "BD," which was for "bottom drawer," because she'd once stepped into an open dresser drawer to reach something on a shelf and fallen over, cutting her lip. And James called Jojo "Speaker," short for "speakerphone," because when she was a baby she used to cry if she heard Uncle Frank's voice but couldn't see him anywhere. The names were kind of mean, but I had secretly wanted a James nickname for a long time.

I couldn't remember doing anything Ping-Pong-related that James might be making fun of me for, but I didn't care. I actually *liked* the name Ping-Pong, until Aunt Ess heard him down at our dock and told him to march himself up to the porch so they could "have a chat."

"Aunt Ess, I don't mind it!" I called after them. But she ignored me.

"You mean you *like* being a Ping-Pong ball?" Angelica said. Angelica is a year and a half older than me. We were trying to teach Jojo, even though she was only five, to play volleyball on the little beach where we kept the boats pulled up next to our dock. Now Angelica was tapping the dirty volleyball with the tips of her fingers. She had it trapped between a hip and an elbow.

"What?" I felt my eyes narrowing. I hated it when I didn't understand something right away.

"You go back and forth, right? From your mom's to your dad's? Like a Ping-Pong ball." She smiled.

I was on top of her in three steps. First, I yanked her ponytail, and then I smacked that ball off her hip, down to the dirt.

"*Bea!*" Aunt Ess shouted down from the porch. I guess she'd been yelling at James and watching over us at the same time.

Angelica just stood there smiling.

I stomped to the water and floated on my back with my ears under the water so that I couldn't hear. Angelica was stuck waiting for me to get out because we were swim buddies. James didn't call me Ping-Pong again. Or anything else.

When my parents were together, two weeks at the lake with my cousins was never enough for me. After the divorce, it felt about a week too long.

It felt too long the summer I was eight, when my cousin Jojo was finally old enough to stay up and play Sorry! with us after dinner. Green is Jojo's favorite color, too, so I let her have my pieces, and I took Mom's blue ones.

It felt too long the summer I was nine. That was the summer the chipped yellow bowl broke. I don't know how it happened; I just saw the pieces in the garbage.

It felt especially too long the summer I was ten. The summer Angelica fell. When those two weeks were finally over, I was in the back seat of our car even before Rocco, our dog, could hurl himself in there. And Rocco loves the car.

News

I like to dance. Not "dance" dance, with mirrors and leotards, but secret dancing in my room with my earbuds in. I don't know how it looks, but I know how it feels. It feels like I know exactly what to do. I know when to turn or sidestep, when to take it easy and when to go a little crazy. It doesn't matter whether I'm at my mom's or at my dad's. I keep my eyes closed, and I'm wherever I'm supposed to be.

But when I'm dancing, I'd rather be at my dad's, because my mom doesn't believe in bedroom-door locks. And she has a way of flinging my door open as if she's trying to catch me at something.

"Bea, you have a fever. You should be *resting*." This was at the beginning of fifth grade, when I was ten. Right after Jesse moved in with Dad and me.

"Mom!" I was breathing hard from dancing.

"What?"

"Privacy?"

She made a face. That's what Mom thinks of privacy.

"Dad just called," Mom said. "Sheila's on her way."

This is all part of the story about the sound of corn growing. Believe it or not.

I'd stayed home sick, so my babysitter, Sheila, was picking me up from Mom's apartment, instead of at school. Sheila picked me up on my "Dad days"—Mondays and Wednesdays and every other Friday. She also used to clean Dad's apartment. And she walked our dog, Rocco.

On Tuesdays and Thursdays and every other Friday, Mom picked me up at school. Mom cleans our apartment herself because she doesn't believe in paying someone else to pick up your mess. Or your dog's.

Dad doesn't believe in ten-year-olds going to PG-13 movies, and Mom doesn't believe in cereal with more than three grams of sugar per serving. Dad doesn't believe in curse words, and Mom doesn't believe in going to school with a temperature above 98.6.

Dad thinks anything below 100 is fine.

Mom doesn't believe in wasting money, but Dad says it's fine to splurge once in a while. When he bought me a puffy purple swivel chair for my room at his apartment, Mom muttered about it, and I went online and found out it cost almost 200 dollars, and after that I felt weird.

Dad believes in allowance for chores. Mom believes in free

allowance and doing chores for nothing. But Dad's allowance is a dollar higher. Confused? Welcome to my life.

Sometimes when I'm dancing at Dad's with the door locked tight, I slam myself into that puffy purple swivel chair and just *spin*. Everything is a blur, and my feet kick off the floor, shooting me around, and around, and around.

At Mom's, I do my spinning on my feet, with my arms stretched out.

The doorbell rang, and I heard Mom let Sheila in. My temperature was only 99.3. Even after a lot of dancing, I couldn't get it up to Dad-sick, so I knew I was going to school the next day. Thursday. Spelling-test day. I looked on my desk for my word sheet.

I picked up my backpack and started throwing stuff in: word sheet, math workbook, planner, colonial-breakfast folder (with butter recipe), and the only barrette I had that actually stayed in my hair. Most of them fall straight down.

Sheila knocked on my bedroom door, and I yelled "Come!" which is what Captain Picard always says on *Star Trek: The Next Generation*. Sheila and I used to watch that show together at Dad's. (Eventually, we streamed all seven seasons. That's a lot of *Star Trek*.)

Anyone would like Sheila—she has pink glasses and big hair, and she wears a lot of bracelets. And cowboy boots, even in summertime.

"You're sick?" Sheila said.

"*Mom*-sick."

She nodded. Sheila got it, even though her parents were never divorced. They stayed married until they died.

"Got your medicine?" Sheila said.

"Yep." I patted my bag.

"Shall I set a course for Ninety-Ninth Street, Captain?"

I tugged down the front of my shirt with both hands. "Make it so!"

Sheila was the one who noticed that Captain Picard was always tugging on his uniform, pulling it down in front like he was trying to cover his stomach. She heard the actor being interviewed on TV, and he said it was because they made the costumes a little too short.

I hugged Mom goodbye.

"I'll see you after school tomorrow," she said, squeezing me. My face was mushed against her, so one ear heard the regular way, and the other one heard through her body. When we let go, I saw her see the rash on my neck, which itched.

"Got your medicine?"

"Yes!" I hated being asked things twice. Even by two different people.

"Don't shout at me, Bea."

"I'm not."

And Sheila said, "Let's go, Captain."

The medicine is for my skin. I have eczema, which you probably haven't heard of. Eczema is where your skin itches in a lot of different places, and when you scratch, you get these sore, rashy patches that people look at and wonder if they're catching. Sometimes people *ask* if they're catching, which is better than whispering about it.

Eczema is not something that you get for a week and then it goes away, like a cold. It's something you have until maybe you grow out of it, like my cousin Angelica's stutter. Also, eczema hurts.

At Dad's, Sheila and I walked Rocco and made grilled cheese sandwiches for dinner. We were about to start an episode of *Star Trek: The Next Generation* when Dad came home.

"You're early!" I told him. Because he doesn't usually get back from the restaurant until later.

Dad came right over to the couch and put his palm flat on my forehead like he was checking for a fever. I waited. Sheila waited. We both knew what he was going to do.

When he took his hand away, he pressed it against his own forehead and looked shocked. "Oh *no*," he said. "I think I have a fever!"

"Dad!"

He kicked off his shoes. "Kidding. But you don't seem hot. Tomorrow's Thursday. Did you guys do spelling?"

Sheila nodded. "I quizzed her."

She did quiz me. I didn't get all the words right, even the third time, but she quizzed me.

"Great." Sometimes Sheila hung out with me and Dad until Jesse got home. But that night she blew me a kiss and left.

*   *   *

In fifth grade, I had a spelling test every Thursday. My teacher, Mr. Home, was a good teacher. Mom said his head was on right. Mom remembers all the teachers she's ever had, starting in first grade. She especially remembers the one who told her she didn't have "a mind for math." Mom became a math teacher. Now she teaches *other* teachers how to teach math.

But even Mr. Home made mistakes. For one thing, he always called my best friend Angus "College Boy," which Angus hated. For another thing, Mr. Home had lunch parties for spelling experts. If you were not a spelling expert, you were not invited.

On the last Friday of every month, Mr. Home invited every kid who got a ten-out-of-ten on all of that month's spelling tests to eat lunch in our classroom instead of the lunchroom. They played the radio, Angus told me, but I wouldn't know about that because I have never gotten a ten-out-of-ten on even *one* spelling test. I told Mom I didn't have "a mind for spelling," but she looked mad and said that I should never say what my mind is not for.

At the beginning of that year, Mom bought these cards that we looked at together, with the rules of spelling on them, like *When two vowels go walking, the first one does the talking.* That means when two vowels are right next to each other, you usually say them like the *first* vowel.

But after I spelled *relief* r-e-l-e-i-f and got another seven-out-of-ten, I told Mom to forget me ever looking at those cards again.

16

I thought Mr. Home should let *everyone* listen to the radio and eat lunch in the classroom on the last Friday of every month. I had written him a long letter about it, in the lunchroom, while everyone was having their first spelling party in September. But it had some bad words, and I didn't give it to him.

After Sheila left, Dad and I watched *Star Trek*.

Then Angus called.

"Are you better now?" Angus hated it when I wasn't in school. We'd been in the same class every year since kindergarten, and he had never missed a day.

"I'm probably better," I said.

"Good." He still sounded annoyed. I smiled.

"We just watched a really good *Star Trek*," I told him. "Captain Picard gets hit by this light beam from a mysterious probe, and it magically transports him to a little planet. He gets totally stuck there. No one from his ship ever comes to get him, and there's no way to get off the planet. After a while, he just has to deal with it. Luckily, it's a really good planet to be on. Everyone is nice. He has this great life there. He's married, and he has kids, and then he gets old and everything. And he learns to play the flute."

"The *flute?*"

"Yeah. But in the end, Captain Picard finds out that he was never on that planet at *all*. The whole thing was happening in his mind. The light beam had some kind of *brain* virus inside it. The people on the planet made the probe and sent it into space because their world was about to explode, and they wanted someone in the universe to know who they were. The planet was already gone. But in his head, Captain Picard lived there for half his *life*. He had grandchildren!"

"So he was on his ship the whole time?" Angus said. "Let me guess—for Captain Picard, in his head, decades went by, but in real life it was only like ten minutes."

Angus really *is* smart enough to go to college.

"Yes!" I said. "He wakes up on the ship and he's in complete shock. When they investigate the probe that hit him with the light beam, all they find is a little box, and inside is a flute. The very end of the episode is Captain Picard, alone, playing the flute while he looks out into space. Missing everyone he thought he knew."

"Wow," Angus said. "That kind of makes me want to cry."

"Yeah." I *did* cry. So you can see why Angus is my best friend.

"See you tomorrow." Angus waited, and then said, *"Right?"*

"Right." I was still thinking about how Captain Picard's brain had grandchildren and learned to play that flute in ten minutes.

It turned out I was lying about seeing Angus at school the next day, but I didn't know it at the time.

After I hung up, Dad sang "Happy Birthday" twice while I brushed my teeth. It wasn't my birthday, but he likes to do that because once, a long time ago, the dentist told me that I should always brush for two rounds of "Happy Birthday," and I told

18

the dentist that it's impossible to sing and brush your teeth at the same time. Dad laughed really hard.

When I was in bed, Dad sat in my purple chair and rolled himself over to me.

"Bea," he said. "I have something to tell you. I hope it'll feel like good news."

"Okay," I said.

"Jesse and I are going to get married."

"Married?"

"Yes." He smiled. "What do you think? I wanted to tell you before he gets home, so you can say whatever you feel like saying."

I had known Dad's boyfriend Jesse for two years already, and he had been living with us for a couple of months. I loved Jesse. But I'd never thought about my dad being *married* to Jesse. Or anyone, except my mom.

After a minute, I said, "It's good, I think. I never want Jesse to leave."

Dad held my hand. "I don't, either, Bea."

After Dad said good night, I went to my backpack and got out my green spiral notebook. The edges of the pages were all curled and dirty. I still carried it everywhere, but I hadn't looked at my list in a long time.

THINGS THAT WILL NOT CHANGE:

1. Mom loves you more than anything, always.
2. Dad loves you more than anything, always.

3. Mom and Dad love each other, but in a different way.

4. You will always have a home with each of us.

5. Your homes will never be far apart.

6. We are still a family, but in a different way.

At the bottom of the list, I added:

23. Jesse is staying.

I got back into bed, not sleepy. After a minute, I jumped up again, leaned into the hallway, and yelled, "Dad! Are we having a *wedding?*"

And Dad yelled back, "You bet we are!"

Jesse

In the beginning, it was hard for me to sleep at Dad's new apartment. I had only lived in one place before. Now it was: Different room. Different bed. Different sounds. No Mom.

Dad bought plants for every window and painted a new rainbow on the wall above my new bed. He bought my little orange couch (for sleepovers), and my puffy purple chair, and my red rug. He bought me new sheets, a new comforter, and two new pillows. He read to me every night.

But at Dad's, I woke up a lot. Sometimes it was my eczema itching. Eczema feels worse at night. But sometimes it wasn't the eczema, and I didn't know what it was. I'd get up and stand in the hall outside Dad's bedroom, holding my pillows and listening to him snore. I liked his snoring. After a while, I'd go in, find the rolled-up sleeping bag under Dad's bed, and spread it out on the floor. I liked the shadows on the ceiling of Dad's room. As soon as I saw those shadows, I felt all right.

That happened a lot of nights. He always left that sleeping bag under his bed so I'd know where to find it. Those first months at Dad's, it was like I had to build a hundred bridges, from me to every new piece of furniture, every new lamp, every new fork, even the bathroom faucets and the lock on the door, until, slowly, all of Dad's new things stopped feeling wrong.

Jesse moved in with us two years later, at the beginning of fifth grade, right before Dad told me about them getting married. The things Jesse brought never felt wrong. They felt like presents.

Jesse brought three old movie posters, a radio, his big blue coffee mug, and an old-fashioned telephone—the kind you dial by sticking your finger in a hole and dragging it. And he also brought his big sister, Sheila, who had already been my baby-sitter for two years. Sheila didn't actually live with us, but once Jesse moved in, she came over a lot. (She still does.) Jesse likes to say that Sheila is a true Southern lady, and every time he does, she winks at me. They grew up in Arkansas, so I guess that means they're both Southern.

Jesse wakes up early. He usually has the radio on when I walk into the kitchen. By the time Dad wakes up, Jesse and I are already eating our double-toast. That's what Jesse calls toast that's buttered on both sides.

Jesse knows it's critical to bring a dessert with your school lunch, even if it's just one little cookie wrapped in a napkin. And he agrees with Mom about not having other people clean up your mess. After he moved in, Sheila stopped cleaning Dad's apartment, and Jesse made us a job wheel for chores, just like the one my all-time favorite teacher, Ms. Adams, had on the wall in second grade. Jesse made one job be "lick floor under table," and that job is always Rocco's.

He loves walking Rocco. Rocco made at least four new dog-park friends the first month Jesse lived with us. I can't even imagine a person (or a dog) who wouldn't want Jesse around.

I'm too old for a babysitter now, but Sheila is still at our place all the time. She says she comes over just to sit on our couch and look at Jesse's happiness. He was a happy kid, she says. But he was a worrier.

I'm a worrier, too. So that makes me love Jesse even more.

Magic

The night Dad told me about getting married to Jesse, my hand itched like crazy and woke me up. It was because of the ring Dad gave me for my tenth birthday that summer, silver with turquoise. My eczema gets bad around that ring.

The apartment was dark, but I could make out Rocco curled up in the hallway between the two bedrooms. I stepped over him and went into the bathroom, where I closed one eye before flipping the light switch.

I held my hand under the faucet and let water run between my fingers, the hotter the better. Hot water on my eczema is the best feeling in the world, like every itch I've ever had in my whole *life* is being scratched in exactly the right spot. But afterward my skin gets dry and itches even more than it did in the first place. And sometimes it bleeds. So I'm not actually supposed to run my hands under hot water. Ever. Mom and Dad say hot water is a "five-second solution" because it only solves the problem for five seconds before making it even worse.

Sometimes those five seconds are hard to resist.

Closing one eye is something Angus showed me. When I shut off the water and flipped the light switch, the bathroom went black. I felt my way into the hall, and I couldn't see anything there, either. But then I opened that closed eye, and I could see. Rocco reappeared on the floor, and I stepped over him again. Angus says it works because that eye stays adjusted to the dark. The first time I tried it, it felt like magic.

Happiness

In the morning, my temperature was 99.0, and my hand was bleeding, just a little, but Dad noticed. He made me take off my turquoise ring and he got out my ointment while I argued about wanting my ring back.

Jesse was sleeping late for once, so I left him a note that said *Congratulations, Dad and Jesse!*

It had one cross-out because first I spelled it *congradulations*. And I drew some wedding things, like flowers and bells. Dad told me the wedding would probably be in May, so I wrote, *MAY!*

"Does Mom know?" I said.

Dad nodded. "Mom and I talked about it yesterday."

I didn't ask what I wanted to, which was *Is Mom sad?*

Dad answered anyway. "She's okay with it, Bea. Really."

When I walked out of Dad's building, I saw the back of Lizette Ford, halfway down the block toward school. Lizette and I got into a big fight in second grade after I sneaked into the coat closet and took a root beer from her lunch bag and put it in *my* lunch bag. I had told Ms. Adams I needed to get my ointment from my backpack because my elbow was itching, but the truth was that I couldn't listen to Lizette bragging about her root beer for one more minute. To make her be quiet, I had announced that *I* happened to have a root beer in my lunch, too. And everyone believed me right away. But then I realized that if I didn't show up with a root beer at lunch, they would all know I had lied. What I needed to do was get a can of root beer before lunchtime, and there was only one place I could think of to find one.

The worst part about taking the root beer was that Ms. Adams was ashamed of me. I had taken Lizette's root beer, and I had lied to Ms. Adams about needing my medicine. *Lied right to my face,* she said. And I loved Ms. Adams. So it was terrible.

But Lizette and I were friends again by the end of that year.

I ran down the block to catch up with her.

"Hey, Bea." She held up a small paper bag by her ear, like she was listening to it. "Where's yours?"

That's when I remembered about the heavy cream. Today was Thursday, and we were making practice butter for our colonial breakfast. Mr. Home was bringing French bread, enough for the whole class, and everyone at table three was supposed to bring a container of heavy cream. The reminder was on the back of the door at Mom's house. But that morning I was at Dad's house, so I didn't see it. Without the reminders, I forgot things. Once I had brought lunch money instead of lunch, thinking it

27

was the day of the zoo trip. Then, on the *actual* zoo-trip day, I forgot again and brought my lunch instead of lunch money. I had to eat my peanut butter sandwich and yogurt raisins while everyone else bought pizza from the zoo cafeteria. Zoo pizza stinks anyway, Angus told me.

I really needed two reminders, one for each house.

"You forgot your cream?" Lizette said.

Table three was the colonial-breakfast food committee. There was also a colonial-breakfast costume committee, a colonial-breakfast decoration committee, a colonial-breakfast invitation committee, a colonial-breakfast play committee, and a colonial-breakfast poster committee.

I nodded, telling myself not to cry. Fifth grade, I reminded myself. *Fifth grade.*

"Let's buy some," Lizette said. She pointed at a deli almost right in front of us, on Broadway.

Lizette was a genius. I had three dollars with me, and she had another dollar in quarters. We were giggling as I counted them out to pay. Then Lizette and I were back on the sidewalk and, not expecting it, I felt . . . *really* happy.

My happiness made me feel huge. I don't know another way to say it. Sometimes my happiness surprises me. I remember the first time it happened. I was little. Mom, Dad, and I were in the car, driving to the lake cabin. When we passed the rusty red bridge that meant we were almost there, I got this giant happy feeling, kind of like I was a balloon, getting bigger and bigger, and so *fast.*

That's how I was feeling when Lizette and I left the store

with my heavy cream. And my huge happiness was what made me do the stupid thing I did next. I saw a big jagged piece of a broken green bottle lying on the sidewalk, and I kicked it. I kicked it from happiness. When my happiness makes me feel huge, it's almost like nothing can hurt me. But I was wearing sandals, and the glass cut my foot.

"Omigosh," Lizette said.

There was blood all over my sandal, filling in the seams where the stitching was. You couldn't even see the cut, there was so much blood. I waited for pain, but none showed up.

"It doesn't hurt," I said. "Let's keep going. The nurse will give me a bandage."

But the nurse also called my mom, who called my dad, who came to get me.

Practice Butter

Two hours later, I was sitting on a stool pulled up to one of the kitchen worktables at Dad's restaurant. I had been to the doctor, and my foot was clean, bandaged, and wrapped in a plastic bag, just in case the health inspector came by.

My dad's a chef, and he has his own little restaurant, which he named after me. Not Bea, which is what people call me. Beatrice. Dad says for the prices he charges, Beatrice works better. My favorite dinner at Dad's restaurant is French toast. It's not on the menu, but he invented a way to make it extra crispy but still magically soft in the middle. I have to eat it in the kitchen. Kids aren't supposed to be eating French toast and doing word-find puzzles in the dining room at Beatrice.

Jesse was hunched over the big reservations book, making notes on a yellow pad. Every day, Jesse called all the people who had reservations to eat at Beatrice the following night. Most people didn't answer their phones. I listened to him leave messages.

Hi, this is Jesse, calling from Beatrice. I'm confirming your reservation for dinner tomorrow night at (whatever) o'clock. If your plans have changed, could you give us a call? Thanks, and we're very much looking forward to seeing you!

Over and over and over. Whenever he said the word *Beatrice,* Jesse made a funny face and pointed at me, which would have made me laugh except I wasn't supposed to, because he had to sound professional.

In between calls, I asked Jesse wedding questions.

Was the wedding definitely going to be in May?

Definitely May.

Where?

They were having it right there, at the restaurant, in the dining room and the back garden.

What about the customers?

The restaurant would be closed that night.

Closed!

Yes. Closed for a special occasion. There would be a sign for the front door.

What was Jesse going to wear?

A suit, probably.

What about Dad?

A suit, probably.

Who was going to be invited?

Everyone!

Would there be a huge cake like on TV?

Absolutely.

Could Rocco come?

Hmm. He had to get back to me on that one.

When his calls were finished, Jesse started opening oysters for the lunch customers. A lot of people eat oysters at Beatrice because there's a special oyster lunch. Jesse talked Dad into it, and now people come from all over the city to eat oysters there.

While I helped Jesse scoop ice onto the round silver oyster trays, I started thinking about how everyone at table three was probably making practice butter right now, and soon they would be eating it on delicious French bread. I could see them in what Miriam calls my "mind's eye." And I could also see the little box of cream I'd bought with Lizette that morning, sitting next to a plastic plant in the nurse's office at school, where I'd left it.

Everyone who knows me agrees that I'm no good at hiding how I feel. Dad says I wear my heart on my sleeve, and that means when I'm sad or mad or happy, you can tell it just by looking at me. Sometimes the person looking at me knows how I feel even before I do. But then I catch up.

When I pictured my carton of cream next to that fake plant in the nurse's office at school, Jesse said, "Bea, what's wrong? You look sad."

Five seconds later, I blurted out, "I'm sad!" And told him the whole story.

"Let's see that recipe," Jesse said.

I got out my colonial-breakfast folder and showed him my butter recipe:

BUTTER

You will need:
1. Heavy cream
2. Empty jar with tight-fitting lid

Instructions:
1. Put cream in jar.
2. Shake jar.*
3. Keep shaking.

*Make sure lid is on tight before shaking!

And because Jesse is Jesse, he went straight to the gigantic Beatrice fridge and found some heavy cream, and we made butter. We used an electric mixer, because Jesse didn't have time to do it by hand, the way the colonists did.

There are four different kinds of bread baked at Beatrice every morning, and I picked my favorite, which is pumpernickel. Jesse cut us each a slice, and we smeared our butter all over them.

Right when I was about to take a bite, Jesse yelled, "Wait!" He reached for a bowl of salt (at Beatrice, they use a lot of salt), and he pinched out a little for each of us, sprinkling it on top.

"*Now.* Ready? On three. One, two ..."

Imagine the most perfect bread and butter in the world.

* * *

On Thursday afternoons, Mom taught the math teachers of the future until two o'clock, and then she picked me up at school and we went to Miriam's office together.

At 2:45, she walked into the restaurant, kissed my plastic-wrapped foot, and gave Jesse a hug. She told him congratulations about getting married, and said yes to a piece of pumpernickel butter-bread.

"Dad told you?" I asked on the way to Miriam's.

She nodded. "It's great, Bea. Right? I mean, Jesse is wonderful. Dad is happy. Are you happy?"

"Yeah. And I guess now Sheila will be like—my aunt?"

"Yes!" she said. "I hadn't even thought of that." I knew Mom liked Sheila. She always gave her a real hug. Mom's face is like mine, though. Her smile was not a hundred percent.

Miriam

Telling a story is harder than I thought it would be. This is mostly about fifth grade, the Year of Dad and Jesse Getting Married, when I was ten.

But certain things happened when I was eight, the Year of Dad Moving Out, which is why I have to keep going back to it. That was also the year I started worrying. It was the year of the three terrible third-grade parties. The year I met Miriam.

If you haven't noticed, I can tell you that I have an excellent memory for things that are not spelling. For instance, I still remember the first conversation I ever had with Miriam. I bet even Miriam doesn't remember that, and she takes notes.

We were on the matching couches near the window in her office, facing each other. I remember being glad that she didn't try to share my couch with me. I wanted my parents to be on my couch, but they were in the waiting room.

She said, "Bea, I'm really glad we're sitting down together. I've been wanting to meet you."

I said, "Why?"

She said, "Because I hear you're a pretty great kid. I like talking to kids. It's part of my work."

I said, "Why?"

She said, "A lot of kids feel good after they talk to me. It helps them sort through some of their feelings."

I said, "Oh. Not me."

She said, "I heard you have a dog, Bea. Your dad told me you went to the animal shelter together to pick him out."

I shrugged. It was weird that she was talking about Rocco. "Is he a big dog, or the little kind?"

I was pretty sure she knew the answer to that question because she seemed to know some things I hadn't told her (I hadn't told her anything), but I said, "Big."

She nodded. "Big dogs are wonderful. I used to have a big dog, too. She was so strong. It wasn't always easy to hold on to her leash. Sometimes I felt kind of pulled around, you know?"

I relaxed a little. "Yeah. Rocco yanks me all over the place when I walk him. And he's still just a puppy. Dad says he might get twice as big."

More nodding. "Want to know something? *Feelings* are sometimes like big dogs, Bea. Sometimes they drag you around a little."

I didn't say anything right away. Then I asked her what happened to her dog.

"What do you mean?" she said.

"You said you *used* to have a dog."

"Oh, yes. Well, she got very old. She was my dog when I was a little girl."

"So she died, right?"

She looked me right in the eye. "Yes. She died."

Then I didn't feel like talking anymore. We played six games of Connect Four instead.

After that first visit, I told Mom and Dad that I was never going back to Miriam's office. I took out my green notebook and, under Things That Will Not Change, I wrote: *I am not going to Miriyems!*

I underlined *not* three times. It's still there in my notebook. Number 14.

Mom and Dad bribed me with sour gummy bears. Every time I went to Miriam's office without complaining (Dad said lucky for me facial expressions didn't count), I got a sticker on a chart on the back of the door at Mom's (because I saw Miriam after school on Thursdays, and Thursday is a Mom day). When I had three stickers, I got a bag of sour gummy bears. Movie-theater size.

At first, I thought Miriam didn't know anything about the gummy bears, but then I found out the whole thing had actually been her idea. One Thursday, after I had started to like Miriam just a little bit, a jar filled with gummy bears showed up on her coffee table between the two couches.

"I hear we both like gummy bears," she said, taking the lid off and pushing the jar toward me.

I said, "Are these even sour?"

Miriam said, "*Super* sour." And she gave me a little wink. After that, the sticker chart at Mom's disappeared. But Miriam kept the jar of gummy bears on the coffee table. She always opened it when we had five minutes left.

A Different Way

You might think that if you were walking down Broadway with a big plastic bag wrapped around your foot inside your (bloody) sandal, people would stare, but I watched all the way to Miriam's and didn't catch one person looking. Mom says that's one of the things she loves about New York City.

Miriam's office is in a regular apartment building that people live in, only she has a special door that leads right from the sidewalk into her waiting room. When we got there, Mom sat on her favorite waiting chair, the one with a little table next to it, and took a folder out of her big bag. It was full of her students' papers to grade, same as usual. I sat across from her and looked at the clock. At 3:30 on the dot, the office door opened and Miriam stuck her head out.

"Bea!" She always said it like that, like she was surprised to see me there.

"Dad and Jesse are *getting married*," I said, sitting down on my couch. "We're having a *wedding*."

"What happened to your foot?" She pointed.

"Did you hear me?"

"Oh, yes! How do you feel about it, Bea?"

"You knew, didn't you?"

"Yes. I knew." Miriam never lies, as far as I can tell. Even that first day, she didn't lie about her dead dog.

"So?" she said. "What do you think?"

I told her I thought it was great, which was the truth. Everything about Dad marrying Jesse felt great. Except for one thing.

"I wonder how my mom feels," I said.

Miriam leaned forward.

"Probably bad," I said. "She probably feels bad."

"Why?"

"Because my mom and dad still love each other." I had already told her how I knew that, from Things That Will Not Change. She'd seen the list.

Mom and Dad love each other, but in a different way.

"You may be right," Miriam said. "She might feel a little sad. But do you think your mom wants your dad to be happy, Bea? She cares about him a lot."

"Yes, I just told you, she loves him. They love *each other*." And right then I felt so sad, saying that. Really sad. I had never cried in Miriam's office, though. I did a lot of talking in there, but my crying switch was off.

"But not in the same way they did when they were married to each other, Bea. They love each other differently now, right?

Like how friends love each other. Or maybe a brother and a sister."

I gave Miriam a look. She knew I had always wanted a sister more than anything, so I didn't know why she would even bring that up.

"Bea?" Her face was a big question mark.

"I don't want to talk about Mom anymore."

"Okay."

We sat there.

"We could talk about what happened to your foot," she said.

So I told Miriam about fifth-grade colonial history, how there was a yearlong project with *research papers* and an *authentic* colonial-breakfast party next April. I told her about practice butter and heavy cream, and kicking the glass from happiness. When I got to that part, she opened the gummy-bear jar and reminded me about *thinking two steps ahead*.

"Poor foot," she said.

Miriam had taught me about *thinking two steps ahead* way back when I was eight, right after I told her about the worst terrible third-grade party, which was Carrie Greenhouse's Halloween party.

We played musical chairs at the party. I didn't care about the prize, which was some stickers, but I also didn't want to lose, because I hated the moment when the music stopped and everyone looked at the person who didn't have a chair. I didn't think I could live through that moment of everyone looking at me and waiting for me to go away. I knew I would get a red face.

When the music stopped the first time, there was an empty chair right in front of me, and so everything was fine. But when the music stopped the second time, the closest chair already had someone sitting in it, someone who was squeezing the seat with both hands. I got really worried then, because even though I didn't have time to look, I guessed all the other chairs were already taken, too. Which meant that, any second now, everyone was going to yell "You're out!"

At me.

Unlike Ben Larson's mom (oops, more about that party later), Carrie Greenhouse's mom talked to my mom right in front of me.

"—and she just—*shoved* him out of the chair. Onto the *floor*."

Mom looked sorry and turned to me. "Bea, did you apologize?"

Carrie's mom said, "I just think it's so important that kids know how to be *uncomfortable* for a second, you know? She needs to learn— Oh, thank *you*! For *coming*!"

We were standing right next to the elevator, and people were streaming by, grabbing party bags from a big basket next to Carrie's apartment door. Jason Feld's little brother cried for a party bag, and Carrie's mom turned away from us, waved at the basket, and said, "Of course he can have one! I got extras, just in case! Of *course* I'm sure!"

Mom squeezed my hand: once, twice, three times.

I. Love. You.

I squeezed hers back: once, twice.

42

How. Much.

And then Mom squeezed mine again, long and hard.

Sooo much.

Carrie's mom turned back to us. "Maybe there's a book you can buy her? My sister is a teacher, and she says this kind of problem doesn't usually get better on its own. *Unfortunately.*"

Yes, even Carrie Greenhouse's horrible mother has a sister.

Mom was polite to her. We got into the elevator. And then, just as the doors were closing, I threw my party bag at Carrie's mom. It hit the wall right behind her, and everything inside—candy corn, mostly—exploded all over the floor.

Later I told Miriam that when I saw that candy flying everywhere, it was like fireworks were going off inside me, but there were *two* kinds of fireworks—one kind felt really bad, like I didn't want to be doing what I was doing, but the other kind felt *good.* Like I was doing *exactly* what I wanted to be doing.

Miriam said that if I had looked *past* the moment I was afraid of, which was moment of not getting a chair when the music stopped, I would have seen that pushing someone off a chair onto the floor was not the best idea, because then everyone looked at me much more.

That's called *thinking two steps ahead.*

And I had hurt someone. Even though I only felt half-bad about the party bag, I did feel sorry about shoving Angus off that chair.

"Shouldn't I feel really bad about *all* of it?" I asked Miriam. "Because"—I waited to feel really bad about making Carrie's mother pick up all that candy corn—"I don't."

"Carrie's mom was humiliating you, Bea. You got angry. That's *normal*. Throwing candy isn't a great way of expressing your feelings, and that's the part that needs to change. But it doesn't make you a bad person." And to prove it, she threw a gummy bear at me.

That was the day Miriam and I became actual friends. She could have taken the gummy bears away, and I would have kept going to see her anyway. But she didn't. She just kept refilling the jar.

Box!

In the waiting room at Miriam's, Mom's head was bent over the papers in her lap. She didn't hear me come in because of Miriam's noisemaker. It hums really loudly so that no one can overhear anyone else's private conversations.

I tiptoed over to Mom and kissed her on the hair. When she looked up, her glasses were crooked. She pulled me onto her lap, and I leaned back against her, like she was my chair.

"Look at those long legs," Mom said. "How did you get to be ten years old?"

I decided to give her a Miriam-type answer: "One day at a time?"

When Mom unlocked our apartment door, Red was standing right inside, meowing his head off.

"Oops," Mom said. "I must have forgotten to feed him this morning." Because Red never comes to the door when we get home. He's the kind of cat who wants you to come and find *him*. And then he'll let you pet him, but only for half a minute.

"Sorry, Red." Mom grabbed his food bag and shook some onto his plate. I refilled his water bowl, and then I opened the refrigerator and yelled "Box!"

That's what Mom and I used to say whenever Dad left us a food package. He came at least two times a week and left stuff in our fridge, as a surprise: rice with vegetables, chicken in lemon sauce, meatballs, cheesy polenta, and so many other things, always packed in containers with reheating instructions scribbled on strips of blue tape across their tops.

The first time Dad left us food was right after he moved out. It was in a big cardboard box, crammed into the fridge, and I yelled "Box!" when I saw it, and pointed. After that, we always yelled "Box!" whether it was actually in a box or not. Then Mom would reheat whatever it was, make a salad, and say, "*Voilà*, dinner!" When there was no box, Mom made us cheese quesadillas, tuna salad with pickles, or scrambled eggs.

"Ooh, what's in there?" Mom said, getting the salad bowl.

It was something big and rectangular. I peeled back the foil. "Looks like . . . lasagna."

"Yum."

"And there's some kind of cake. Lemon cake!" I know the shape of Dad's lemon cake because he always uses this one pan with ridges on top.

"Wow," Mom said. "Cake and everything."

I was unwinding the plastic bag from my foot when the doorbell rang. I hopped over. It was Lizette, holding a greasy paper bag.

"Aw, gross!" Lizette said, pointing. A little blood had soaked through the bandage. I hadn't noticed. She leaned down and yanked off the last piece of plastic, still stuck to my leg with some tape. "I'm glad you're okay, Bea." Then she held out the bag. "Here's what you missed. It was *awful.*"

I took the bag. Inside was a chunk of rock-hard French bread. I tried to bite it, but my teeth just slid off.

"Told you." She did her cat smile. Lizette has two smiles, cat and clown. Cat smile is like she knows something, and clown smile is just goofy. Angus came up with the names. When I asked him what my smiles were called, he said I have too many different ones and he couldn't keep track of them.

Mom invited Lizette to stay for dinner. We had a "working dance party," which Mom invented. It's when you do chores and dance at the same time. It can be for folding laundry or vacuuming or whatever you want. Mom cranked the radio and we unloaded the dishwasher, took turns with the salad spinner to dry the lettuce, and set the table. Mom kept doing hip bumps with us, which I was used to, but which made Lizette laugh until she was almost hysterical. Actual tears were coming down her face.

When the lasagna was hot, Mom turned the radio down and we sat at the table in the kitchen.

"I like dinner at your house," Lizette said. She pointed her fork at her plate. "And this is *so* good."

Mom smiled. "Thank you, Lizette."

Neither of us said that Dad had made it.

While we waited in my room for her dad to pick her up, I told Lizette about Dad and Jesse getting married.

"Ooh, can I come to the wedding?" Lizette said.

I remembered what Jesse had said about who was invited: *Everyone!*

And I told Lizette, "Definitely."

"Will your mom be there?" she asked.

"Of course," I said.

"Oh, I just wondered. I mean—she was married to your dad before, right? It could be awkward."

"My parents aren't like that. They still love each other. In a way." *A different way.*

"That's cool, Bea. You're lucky."

"Yeah."

"My brother has this friend? His parents got divorced, and they are *so* mean to each other."

Lizette has a brother who's three years older than us. He's nice. When Lizette and I were in kindergarten, he was my reading buddy. I remember that she always ran to hug him when he came into our classroom.

"You're lucky, too," I said. "Luckier."

"What do you mean?"

"Because your parents are together. And you have Damian."

"Yeah. But you have your mom, your dad, *and* Jesse. And

Sheila. And a restaurant where you can eat anything you want, anytime you want it!"

That's not actually true. It's not like I can just walk in to Beatrice and order French fries and an ice cream sundae. But I didn't say so.

"Plus," she said, "Damian is allergic to animals. So I can't have a cat *or* a dog. You have both."

Right then, her dad rang our bell. Lizette smiled (clown smile) and bounced off the bed.

When she was gone, I found Mom loading the dishwasher. No music.

I said, "You're coming to the wedding, right?"

She looked surprised. "I haven't even thought about it."

"I want you to come," I said.

She nodded. "In that case, I will be there with bells on."

"Okay. But you don't need to bring bells. Jesse says Sheila is doing the decorations."

She told me it's an expression. It just means she's going to get dressed up.

Then she turned the radio on.

I didn't think she wanted to dance, so I went to my room to worry.

Drop Everything and Worry

My dad almost choked to death once, on an orange. It was a long time ago, before the divorce. He'd shoved a few sections in his mouth (it was maybe a quarter of an orange, he told me later), and then he couldn't breathe. He started running around the apartment in a panic. Mom wasn't home. I didn't know what to do, and even if I had known, I wasn't strong enough to do it. Dad rushed out of our apartment and banged on our neighbor's door. The neighbor realized right away what was wrong and did the Heimlich maneuver on Dad. The orange popped out of his windpipe and flew across the hall, where it landed on Mrs. Carmody's doormat, which says "Welcome" in ten languages. (Angus has memorized them all.)

The neighbor was Jesse. He wasn't our neighbor, really—he was cat-sitting for our actual neighbor, who was in California. It was really lucky Jesse was there, because our actual neighbor is a lawyer who is almost never home, and Dad might have died right on his doorstep. Now that I think about it, I don't even know why that lawyer got a cat in the first place.

After the orange hunk landed on the doormat, the hallway was quiet for a few seconds except for the sound of my sobbing. All I did the whole time until Jesse saved Dad was scream, and all I did afterward was cry. This was back when I wasn't so great in emergencies. But I was only seven.

The lawyer's cat ran out between Jesse's legs and walked around sniffing everybody's doormats while Dad thanked Jesse about a hundred times. The next day he made Jesse a coffee cake. They became friends. When the lawyer came home, Jesse left. But Dad and Jesse stayed friends. When Dad moved out, Jesse's big sister, Sheila, started babysitting for me and cleaning up for Dad. After a while, Dad and Jesse fell in love.

Angus asked me once if I thought my dad "turned gay" when he choked on that orange. But Dad said no, that being gay had been a part of who he was from the beginning of his life. The orange just showed him how short life could be.

After I saw Dad almost choke to death, I had a worrying problem. I started to worry all the time. I worried that one of my parents would die while I was at school. I worried that I would die while I was at school. If I fell and scraped my knee, I worried that all my blood would fall out of my body.

One of the first things Miriam told me about was how to worry. She wanted me to worry for five minutes straight, two times a day. She said I should sit quietly somewhere, maybe with a piece of paper and some colored pencils, and just *worry*, one time in the morning and once at night (but not right before bed). And if my worry showed up at any other time, like during school or at Angus's house, Miriam said I should tell it, "Go away, and I'll see you later."

It actually works. Sitting down to worry on purpose is kind of like sweeping the wood floor at the lake cabin (which I have always loved to do). Everything ends up in two big piles that I can step around (instead of walking around with sand stuck to my feet all the time, which I hate).

By the time I was ten, I only needed to worry once a day. Usually I worried around dinnertime. After Lizette went home, I sat on my bed and worried about spelling (mostly about the party, not the spelling itself) and I worried about Mom.

Angus called right after I finished.

"Did you get stitches?"

"No. Just a bandage." Angus knew that "stitches" was on my list of nightmares. Angus's number one nightmare was eating a scallop.

"Lizette said there was blood all over."

"There *was* blood all over." Some kids might have wanted to see that, but Angus was not one of them.

"Are you coming back to school tomorrow?"

"Yep. How was the spelling test?"

"Easy." Then he felt bad. "I mean—"

"It's okay. How was the practice butter?"

I could hear him make a face, don't ask me how. "Pretty gross," he said.

"Yeah, Lizette brought me some."

"She did? It tasted like nothing. No one brought salt."

I pulled out my folder. "The recipe doesn't *say* salt," I said, thinking of Jesse and his bowl of salt. "Maybe the colonists didn't have salt?"

"Well, they didn't have French bread, either. Mr. Home says he's going to bring salt next time."

In the morning, I sat on the edge of the bathtub and soaked my foot while Mom quizzed me on times tables, which I knew perfectly. Then she patted my foot dry with a clean towel. The cut looked tiny. One Band-Aid covered it.

At school, Mr. Home said I could take yesterday's spelling test right after lunch, during Drop Everything and Read. He scored it right in front of me, and I got a seven out of ten. At the top of the paper, he wrote *Not bad!* and drew a smiley face. It was only the first week in October, and I was already uninvited to the next radio party.

The Second Family Meeting

That weekend was a Dad weekend (the weekend = Friday and Saturday), so Sheila picked me up after school on Friday to take me to Dad's.

"Rough week!" she said. "Fever and injury! How's your foot?"

"It's fine." I waved it around in a circle. Mom had made me wear sneakers and socks, so there was nothing to see.

"You're good to walk?"

I nodded.

She said, "You heard about the wedding?"

"Yep. In May!"

Sheila grinned at me. "You know what's great about May?"

I couldn't think of anything. "What?"

She held her hand up for a high five. "The wedding!"

"You're weird," I told her. But I high-fived her anyway.

When we got to Dad's, I let my backpack slide to the floor, hugged Rocco, and said, "*Star Trek?*"

She smiled. "I'm leaving early today, Bea."

"You are?" Dad and Jesse usually came home *extra* late on Fridays.

I noticed a smell. Popcorn?

"Surprise!" Dad practically jumped out of the kitchen with a giant bowl of popcorn.

Sheila kissed me on the cheek. "See you next week."

"Parmesan popcorn!" Dad said. Then he told me that Jesse was on his way home, and that we were having a family meeting.

A family meeting.

Right away I figured the wedding was off. I didn't understand why Dad was bothering with popcorn, because how could I be in the mood for Parmesan popcorn if Dad and Jesse were getting divorced before they even got married in the first place?

I locked my bedroom door and spun around in my purple chair until I felt sick. It took Jesse forever to get home.

We sat in the living room. I wondered if I would get another spiral notebook. Dad put the popcorn on the table next to the couch and I ignored it.

And then Dad and Jesse said the single best thing anyone could ever say to anyone: I was getting a sister.

Jesse's daughter, Sonia, who lives in California, was coming to stay with us, for a week.

"I want Sonia to start spending some time with us in New

York," Jesse said. "In the summertime, and on school vacations. I want you two to get to know each other. After the wedding, you'll be sisters."

Jesse had told me about Sonia. I'd seen pictures of a dark-haired girl, usually in a sundress. I knew we were both in fifth grade. I knew he went to visit her in California a few times a year. I knew he called her on the phone. But Jesse never once talked about Sonia coming to stay with us. For some reason, it never even occurred to me that this was possible. And I had never thought about how *Dad and Jesse getting married meant I was going to have a sister.* And now she was coming to live with us (for a week). *Soon.*

A sister. I was finally getting a sister. Not only that, but she was staying in my room, with me, for a whole week. And it turned out that we practically had the same birthday.

"*June?*" I shouted.

"Yes!" Jesse shouted. Another thing I love about Jesse: if you get excited and shout, he gets excited and shouts. "You guys are only twenty-two days apart!"

I hit the couch with my fists. "Why couldn't we have been born on the same day? Then we'd be twins!"

Dad reached for my hand and said, "Thanks for being so terrific about this, honey."

I was way too excited to hold Dad's hand. I was getting a sister. She was going to *share my room for seven days.* What was there to be terrific *about?* The whole *thing* was terrific!

"I'm going to clean my room," I said. "I mean, *our* room."

I locked my door and dance-cleaned my room.

Dancing, I got all the dirty clothes off my floor and into my laundry basket. I made my bed. Still dancing, I rearranged my jewelry box, lining up my turquoise ring, my three bracelets, and my yellow cat pin. I looked at the orange couch, where Sonia would sleep. I got the lint roller and rolled it all over the couch. I hoped Sonia wasn't allergic to dogs like Lizette's brother. I shook the big square pillows so they looked puffier.

Then I stood in the middle of the room, breathing hard. I wiggled my bad foot, hoping I hadn't opened the cut. I checked the Band-Aid, and it looked okay. But my room still didn't look right.

I dragged the couch over to my bed, one corner at a time, my arms shaking, until the couch and the bed were lined up perfectly, like the orphans' beds in *Madeline*, which had been my favorite book for at least two years when I was little.

Dad knocked, and I opened the door.

"Bea—um, you moved the couch by yourself?"

"Yeah. It's not heavy."

He nodded, looking. Thinking. "Sonia's not coming until January. You heard that part, right?"

"Dad?"

"Yes?"

"Can I have some privacy?"

He blinked. "Oh. Sure."

I locked the door after him, put my headphones on, and danced.

"So what's her name?" Angus asked on the phone that night.

I smiled. "Sonia. Good name, right?"

"It's a nice name. But it isn't as nice as Beatrice."

I said, "Oh, yes, it is."

"Sonia is great," Sheila said when she picked me up after school on Monday. "I'm so happy she's coming, Bea. This is just— wonderful."

"A *real* sister," I reminded her. "When Dad and Jesse get married, we'll be *legally* sisters. Just like sisters anywhere."

Sheila squeezed my arm. Her bracelets jingled. "She's lucky to be getting you as a sister."

"I'm lucky, too," I told her. "Luckier."

What If

Miriam said that I should try to think of *all the possibilities* about what might happen when Sonia came. She said I should think about what it might feel like for Sonia, getting on a plane and flying all the way across America to her dad's new family.

I reminded Miriam that I have been on a plane by myself, to Florida. Dad was already there for a food-festival job, and I was meeting him afterward for a vacation. Mom took me to the airport on the M60 bus. An airline lady gave me a big orange sticker to wear on my shirt. It said, "I'm Flying Solo!" and Mom came with me right up to the door of the plane to say goodbye, and then I sat next to a woman who had a tiny dog in a bag between her feet. I didn't even know that dog was there until the very end, after we landed, when she held him up to look out the window. I guess she was showing him Florida.

The worst part of the whole trip was that the flight attendant told me she had a special treat for me, which turned out to be a hot dog. I hate even looking at a hot dog, and I *really* hate smelling a hot dog, but she said the pilot had asked for that hot dog to be put on the plane *especially for me*, and she certainly hoped I was going to eat it. And then, for some reason I still don't understand, I *did* eat it.

After she took my empty tray, I stared straight ahead for the rest of the trip. When we landed and the plane door finally opened, all of this sticky air came in. We lined up and walked out, and there was Dad, standing next to some empty chairs in the Florida airport. As soon as I saw him, I threw up all over the rug, and then I started crying.

Dad said I should have told the flight attendant, "No, thank you."

I made a reminder in my head for Jesse to tell Sonia about saying "no, thank you" if she doesn't like the food on the plane.

Then Miriam said that when she suggested I think about how Sonia might feel about the trip, she didn't just mean the *plane trip*, but the whole idea of what the trip meant: That Sonia's dad was getting married to my dad. That Dad and Jesse and I were living together now, as a family.

"On Mondays and Wednesdays," I said.

"Right," Miriam said.

"And every other weekend."

"Yes," Miriam said, "but are you thinking about what I'm saying, Bea? It might take Sonia a while to get used to the idea of her father getting married again. What if she's never been so far from her mom before? What if she feels uncomfortable or strange for a while? Let's make a list of all the different things Sonia might feel. Can you start?"

"She might feel excited and happy," I said. "Because now she has a sister almost exactly her age."

Miriam nodded. "And she might feel excited and happy and *quiet*. Or *not sure how she feels*. She might feel homesick."

I noticed that all of Miriam's ideas were bad ones. "You went three times in a row," I said.

Miriam said, "You're right. I apologize."

"Sonia might feel *lucky*," I said. "Because she'll have a sister, which she didn't have before. And, I just realized, she has a dog now, too—she has Rocco! Maybe she wants a sister just as much as I do. Or even more." I wasn't sure that was possible.

Miriam smiled. "Yes. Or she might not know right away how she feels about a new sister."

"Until she meets me," I said.

The October Spelling Party

I hate today," I told Mom before school on the last Friday in October.

I'm always at Mom's on spelling-party mornings, because the parties are on Fridays, and I'm at Mom's on Thursday nights (Thursday = Mom day).

Mom said getting mad about the spelling parties was understandable, but that I should also think about whether I could make myself feel better by doing "something special."

"I can't *do* anything," I told her. "I have to sit in the dumb lunchroom! And dumb Carolyn Shattuck always sits next to me!" Carolyn Shattuck couldn't spell, either. But that wasn't what I meant by dumb.

"Maybe we can pack something special in your lunch," Mom said. "Maybe you can bring your puzzle book and do all the word-finds." The word-finds were my favorite kind of puzzle. I loved circling the words.

"Wait!" I said. "What if I write a letter to Sonia in the lunchroom? We can be pen pals." Because January was still far away. I wanted to know Sonia faster.

"Great idea," Mom said.

I kept my "B" stationery at Mom's, which was lucky. I ran to my room to get it. Every page had a big, curly *B* at the top, and the envelopes were covered in stars. Mom had given it to me for my birthday, and I only used it for special occasions. Carefully, I slid two pieces of stationery and one envelope into my homework folder.

When it was time for lunch, Mr. Home said that kids eating in the lunchroom should line up as usual. This was the worst part of it, having to line up while everybody looked. I grabbed my homework folder and held it close to me, like it was important. I also tried to look like I was thinking about something interesting, something so interesting I never even noticed that most of the class wasn't lining up.

What I forgot to do was get my lunch from the coat closet. So I had plenty of time to write my first letter to Sonia.

Another thing I have noticed about telling a story is that spelling mistakes are not interesting. In fifth grade, my letters were full of spelling mistakes, but I am not going to put them in.

B

Dear Sonia,

How are you? I'm in the lunchroom at my school. Half my class gets to eat in our classroom today with the radio playing, but not me, and not Carolyn Shattuck, who is sitting right next to me, even though I purposely left my sweatshirt there. She just slid it over. Do you have annoying people in your class this year?

My best friends are Angus and Lizette. You can meet them when you come. Lizette has a brother who's three years older, and Angus has a sister in college already! I know you have two little brothers. What are their names? Are they annoying? Or not?

When we were in second grade, Carolyn Shattuck told me to make a bridge with my pencil between my hands. She wanted to karate-chop it. But instead of breaking in half like it was supposed to, the pencil stabbed me right under my thumb, and I had to go to the nurse. When the cut healed, there was a pencil mark that never went away. My dad calls it the world's tiniest tattoo.

Write me back if you can.

Your future sister,

Bea

The November Spelling Party

Dear Sonia,

My teacher, Mr. Home, started a new thing. When he hands back our spelling tests, he balances them on our heads. If we can keep them there until he gets back to his desk, we get a plus-one on the test. Everyone gets a plus-one, because he lets us cheat by holding the papers on our heads with our hands. Now even more people get invitations to the spelling parties, but I am still not one of them. My mom put a cranberry muffin and two caramels in my lunch today because she knows that spelling-party Fridays are the worst.

I got your postcard. California looks cool. It's good that your brothers are not annoying.

This week at school we started a project called "my

breakfast table." It's because we're doing colonial America this year. In April, all the parents are coming to our colonial breakfast. I'm on the food committee with Lizette and Angus. We're making butter from scratch. It takes forever!

For "my breakfast table," we're supposed to think about how we have breakfast in modern times, like what we eat and where everyone sits and everything. We have to draw diagrams on graph paper and label them. I have two tables, one at my mom's and one at my dad's, so I'm doing two diagrams. Maybe I will get extra credit.

Your future sister,

Bea

The December Spelling Party

Dear Sonia,

Thanks for postcard number two! Do you have any stationery? Then you could fit more words. My Thanksgiving was good, too. Mom and I went to my dad's restaurant, like always. Dad and Jesse (your dad!) came and sat with us whenever they got work breaks. Sheila (your aunt!) came, too. A lot of people go to restaurants on Thanksgiving, did you know that? That's why my dad always has to work.

After we ate, I helped in the coat room while my mom and Sheila talked. There are three coats in the coat room that people left behind a long time ago. They are always there, even when the restaurant is closed. Angus calls them the orphan coats, and he named them

Gerald, Phoebe, and Tim. Whenever Angus comes to the restaurant, he visits them and shakes their sleeves like they're people. It's pretty funny.

I finished the "my breakfast table" project. When I showed Mr. Home my diagrams, he told me his parents got divorced, too, when he was thirteen.

My mom's kitchen table is round, with three chairs. Dad's table is rectangular. I labeled one chair "Jesse." It's the chair he always sits on. You'll see. I told Mr. Home all about how our dads are getting married, and I also told him about you. We have a fourth chair at Dad's, if you are wondering. We actually have six. I also put an arrow pointing under the table, and wrote "Rocco." Jesse told me you know about Rocco already. But did he tell you that Rocco really likes to be under the table while we eat?

Carolyn Shattuck (remember her?) keeps trying to read my letter! She is so annoying. She made me look at her diagram. She has a brother now because her mom got married again and had a baby. Carolyn labeled his chair "highchair," and his breakfast food is "gross banana mush." I wish she could get 10s on her spelling tests, even if I never will. Then she could go to Mr. Home's radio parties and leave me alone.

Angus's breakfast diagram looks like this: a rectangle labeled "Angus" (this is his bed, with him in it) and, right next to it, a circle labeled "brownie" (this is his breakfast). Angus had a big fight with his

68

mom about his "fundamental human right" to save his dessert for breakfast. Angus won. So now he sits up in bed every morning and the first thing he does is eat yesterday's dessert. But he doesn't get to have dessert after dinner. I don't know if I would make that trade.

Mr. Home loves Angus's diagram so much he asked to make a copy.

We made practice butter again this week. It turned out better than the first time.

This is the longest letter I ever wrote!

Your future sister,

Bea

P.S. Your aunt Sheila says that if you get a shiver for no reason it means that someone is walking on your future grave. Do you believe that?

January (Finally)

Sonia and I have a lot in common. Our parents are divorced. Our dads are gay. We both love barbecue potato chips. And yogurt with tons of honey. We agree that pistachios are the best of all the nuts. But she is different from me in at least one way, which is that you can't tell how she's feeling just by looking at her. At all.

On our first night together, after Sonia put her blue suitcase in my room, after I showed her the two drawers I had cleared out for her, asked her which of my stuffed animals she wanted to sleep with, and made Rocco shake hands with her three times, Dad and Jesse took us out to eat at Pizzeria Pete's, where there's unlimited refills on soda. Usually Dad lets me have zero sodas, but he said tonight the rules were "out the window."

I told Sonia about the just-a-little-bit-burnt crusts at Pizzeria Pete's, how they are the most delicious when you dip them in the ranch salad dressing, and I warned her to hide her crusts from Dad and Jesse, who will just take them without even asking. We ate our pizza and saved our crusts in our laps while Dad pretended to look everywhere for burnt crusts and be sad when there were none, and Sonia laughed really hard. Her hair bounced on her shoulders the way I always wished mine would, but I wasn't jealous because Sonia was going to be my sister, so it was like that hair was already a little bit mine.

Sonia and I each had two sodas, first a root beer and then a ginger ale. She was smiling a lot, and I said to myself that Miriam was wrong to worry about her so much. Sonia smiled right up until the moment she ran away from the table and out the front door of Pizzeria Pete's.

Jesse jumped up, grabbed Sonia's coat from the back of her chair, and ran after her.

Dad looked at me, and his eyes were tired. "Sonia's having a little bit of a hard time—for one thing, I think she's exhausted."

"But she was happy," I said. "She *looked* happy."

"I know, sweetie." Dad didn't look happy.

We sat there.

He said, "Sonia has never been so far away from her mom before, Bea. The idea of spending time with two families is all new for her. It's not easy."

I didn't say anything.

He said, "Hi."

"Hi" is our code for a check-in. Miriam taught it to all three of us—me, Mom, and Dad—when they first got divorced. "Hi" means, "I want to know what's going on with you if you want to tell me." It means, "I'm listening."

"Sonia doesn't want to be my sister," I said. "That's mean."

Dad waited.

"She's the meanest person I ever met."

Dad's eyebrows went up.

Then I said, "Miriam says Sonia might get homesick."

"I think that's what's happening," Dad said. "Think about it, Bea. Her parents live on opposite sides of the country. If she's with one of them, she's very far from the other."

"I would hate it if you and Mom lived far apart," I said. And right then I missed Mom so much. Which happens a lot.

"I would hate that, too," Dad said.

My parents will always live close to each other. It's on the list of Things That Will Not Change. So I didn't have to worry about that.

My plan had been to wait for Sonia to come back to the table and then I'd stomp off to the bathroom, to show her exactly how mad I was that she didn't want to be my sister. I put a cancel on that plan.

"Can't Sonia's mom move to New York?" I said. "And then Sonia could live with us on Mondays and Wednesdays. And every other weekend. And every other Sunday."

I let myself think about that. My room at Dad's would be *our* room, for real. She'd have her own bed, and it would look just like mine. Maybe our comforters would match.

Dad smiled. "Sonia's mom is remarried. Sonia has two little brothers."

"I *know*," I said. She didn't have a sister, though. Yet.

"They have jobs in California," he said. "It's where they want to live. The same way we want to be here."

Dad was looking at something behind me, and I twisted around to see Jesse and Sonia hugging next to the cash register. It was a long hug.

I had two pizza crusts hidden under my napkin. I gave Dad one of them, and he just held it. So I just held the other one.

Miriam taught us the Rule of Hi after Ben Larson's eighth birthday party, which was one of the three terrible third-grade parties. Ben invited the whole class for a speedboat ride in the Hudson River. The driver made the boat go *super* fast, and I thought we might all get dumped off the back, into the river, like garbage gets dumped out of a garbage truck.

I screamed, "I don't like this!" again and again until the ride was over, because I had the idea that my screams were protecting me (and everyone else in the boat) from drowning. After a while, I got really tired of screaming, but I always told myself, "One more."

By the time Mom came to pick me up from the playground where we sang "Happy Birthday" and ate Ben's cake, I had pretty much forgotten about the whole thing, but Ben's mom hadn't. She took my mom over to a tree and talked to her. I could see Mom nodding.

"You didn't like the boat ride, huh?" Mom asked me on the way to the subway. She had her hand on my shoulder.

"I hated it," I said.

Miriam says that, a lot of the time, behind the feeling "I hate this" are *other* feelings. Like maybe "I'm afraid of this" is hiding behind "I hate this." And maybe hiding behind "I'm afraid of this" is "I don't know what's going to happen next" or "I don't know if I can do this." There are a lot of feelings behind feelings.

When Miriam first told me about that, I got a picture in my mind's eye of a girl standing very still, with someone hiding behind her, and someone *else* behind *her*. And they're all perfectly straight so that no one can tell how many people are actually there. Sometimes I feel exactly like that. Like I'm a bunch of different Beas, all lined up to look like one. I wondered if Sonia ever felt that way. But I didn't know how to ask her.

Sisters

After Pizzeria Pete's, we went home and Sonia Skyped with her mom and her little brothers. She called her mom's husband Dad. I looked at Jesse, but he acted like he hadn't heard it.

In my bedroom, Sonia still hadn't put her clothes in the bureau. They were in her suitcase next to the orange couch, which was all the way across the room again, against the wall. Jesse and Dad had made up the couch like a bed, with two pillows and a little lamp next to it.

Sonia went into the bathroom and came out wearing her nightgown and holding the clothes she'd worn that day, all rolled up into a little ball that she stuffed into her suitcase.

"Use my laundry basket." I pointed to it. "Dad can wash everything together!"

"That's okay," Sonia said. "It's only seven days. I brought enough stuff."

It felt like Sonia was trying to make it sound like this trip was no big deal.

She got under the covers on the orange couch. She turned off her lamp and closed her eyes.

I bounced on my bed, hinting that we didn't have to go right to sleep if we didn't want to. "I'm glad you're here," I said.

I waited a long time for her to say something back, but she didn't. I told myself maybe she just fell asleep.

Miriam says don't lie down inside a bad feeling if you can help it.

When Dad and Jesse told me that Sonia was coming, I asked Mom if I could spend the whole week at Dad's, because Sonia was only staying for six nights and I didn't want to miss any of them. Mom's face changed, but right away she said, "Okay, sweetie, sure." And a second later, she said, "That sounds like fun!"

And right away I felt horrible.

When I feel guilty, it's like a wave is rushing up on me from the ground. First, my legs feel seasick, and then the feeling runs all the way to my head. I wouldn't know this except one time Miriam gave me the homework "What does a feeling feel like?"

She told me to write down where I felt my feelings in my body. I told her that was pretty dumb homework, because feelings didn't feel like anything in my body. "Feelings are in your head," I said. "You don't know you're sad because your *toes* hurt." And Miriam just smiled and said we would talk about it next time.

So I went home and sat on my bed with my green pen and my green spiral notebook, and I thought about what a feeling feels like. First, I thought about Ben Larson's birthday party and the horrible speedboat ride. Right away, my chest hurt like someone was pressing on it and squeezing my throat a little bit at the same time. I wrote in my notebook: *Afraid = throat closes up.* No wonder it had been so hard to scream.

Then I thought about the time I took Lizette's root beer and pretended it was mine, and how Ms. Adams was ashamed of me, and how guilty I felt. It took me five or six times of thinking about that to write down exactly where the seasick feeling starts (in my legs), how it goes through my stomach and the wrong way up my throat, and how, when it gets to the top of my head, it fizzes.

It's worse when I don't expect it. When I told Mom I wanted to spend a whole week with Dad and Jesse because I was getting a sister, I didn't know it would hurt her feelings until I saw the way she looked right *before* she said, "That sounds like fun!" The fizzing in my head lasted longer than usual, almost like a burn.

In the middle of Sonia's first night, I woke up because my hand was itching and the backs of my knees were stinging. I usually put on lotion before bed, but I didn't want Sonia to see my eczema, so I had skipped it.

According to my digital clock, I scratched for about ten minutes while I listened to Sonia sleep. Then I decided to go to the bathroom to get my medicine. Once I was in there (with one eye open), I held my hand under hot water for just *ten seconds,* to see if it would stop the itching long enough for me to go back to sleep. I hated being the only person awake because it made me lonely. You might think a person can't get lonely that fast, but I can. I wanted to get back to sleeping as fast as I could.

With my one eye, I saw the bathroom door, which I hadn't closed all the way, opening wide, and then Dad was there, blinking in the light. He turned off the hot water and pressed my hand into a towel, his hands flat on the sides of mine. Then he opened the cabinet for my ointment, which he put on the right places between my fingers and on my palm. I did the backs of my knees myself. Dad said, "Hot water is a five-second solution, Bea. Remember? It never lasts. Use the medicine." He put the tube of ointment away and left.

When I turned off the bathroom light, the apartment went dark, but then I opened my closed eye and I saw everything.

Sisters

I have an old-fashioned tape recorder that used to belong to my grandpa—my dad's dad. It still works, with D batteries. When Dad was little, *his* dad read to him at night and recorded the stories so that Dad could hear them again whenever he wanted. When I was little, Dad and I listened to some of them together. Now I listen by myself. I never met my grandpa, because he died when my mom was pregnant with me.

I had never told anyone about those tapes before, not even Angus. My grandpa had this voice, sort of slow and careful but with a big smile in it. It was like Dad had shared that voice with me, and I was helping him keep it.

On her second night with us, I let Sonia listen to my grandpa's very first story tape. I know it was the first one because he wrote dates on all the labels. This one said: *3/8/1983, Frog and Toad.*

Sonia had slept really late that morning, and Dad wouldn't

let me wake her up. Then he made chicken tacos for lunch, and the four of us bundled up and took Rocco for a long walk in the park, where Jesse introduced Sonia to all of Rocco's dog friends (and their owners). Everything was really good until Sonia Skyped with her mom after dinner. Then she did a bunch of crying in the bathroom. I was so afraid she would go home.

Now she was on the orange couch in my room, and I was back in my bed against the opposite wall. The lights were off, and we were listening to my grandpa read *Frog and Toad*. It felt like a relief, because I was getting tired of asking Sonia questions. I'd asked her every question I could think of, which was how I knew that she loves barbecue potato chips and yogurt with honey, that her brothers' middle names are Manuel and Raphael, that she has her own room at home, that she likes to swim, and that she's a good speller. Sonia didn't ask me any questions back.

I'd heard my grandpa read the *Frog and Toad* stories fifty times and never cried before, but for some reason as soon as he began that night, tears started. It was really quiet crying, and I kind of pressed it down with my hands under the covers, which helped me be even quieter, because I didn't want Sonia to know.

I was sad that Sonia didn't want to be there, but I was also happy that she *was* there. I was thinking about the next four nights with Sonia at Dad's, a staircase of happiness in front of me.

My bedroom door opened just a little, and some light fell on the floor. Dad leaned in, and I watched his hand on the doorknob, hoping he wouldn't open the door any more, because the light broke the spell of Grandpa's voice in the dark. Dad listened for a second, and then he closed the door, very quietly.

We got to the end of *Frog and Toad*, and then I swallowed a couple of times and said, "I'm really happy you're going to be my sister." I was afraid of what Sonia might say back. She might say nothing. She might say *We won't really be sisters.* She might have fallen asleep during *Frog and Toad.* That happened to me a lot, actually.

But she answered right away. She said, "Yeah. Can we put in another tape? How many are there?"

A tiny balloon of happiness blew up inside me. I said, "There are a lot."

Sisters

At Miriam's that week, I told her about everything that Sonia and I had in common.

I told her how we'd gone to the museum to look at the armor, which is my favorite thing there, and how Sonia said it was her favorite thing, too, even though she had never been to the museum before. Jesse asked us which was our favorite armor, and we both picked the German armor "for man and horse." Jesse thought it probably weighed a hundred pounds, but Sonia said it was worth it because if you were wearing that, nothing could get you. Or your horse.

Miriam listened.

I told her how Dad wouldn't let me take any days off from school even though Sonia was only there for *one week*, and how Sonia and Sheila had made cookies together and gone shopping without me, which made me feel left out until I came home and found a big cookie and a pair of very cool barrettes on my pillow. I told her how Sonia was spending time at the restaurant with Jesse and Dad, and that Angus and I went after school one day to meet them there. Angus introduced Sonia to the orphan coats (Gerald, Phoebe, and Tim). He made her shake hands with their sleeves, and she laughed really hard and said two times how lucky I am that a restaurant is named after me. We all stayed for family meal, which everyone working at Beatrice eats together at four o'clock every day, before the dinner rush starts. (Angus loves family meal. He loves that it's loud, and that you're allowed to eat standing up.) Then Jesse made a special dessert, just for me, Angus, and Sonia, which turned out to be warm peanut-butter cookies with chocolate chips and whipped cream on top.

Miriam listened.

I told her how every dinner was fun this week because Dad and Jesse came home early and bedtime was "out the window," and how Sheila brought over some amazing ice cream bars and Sonia and I both ate all the chocolate off ours first. And how we laughed when we realized.

When we had five minutes left, Miriam opened the gummy-bear jar and put it between us on the coffee table. The jar was filled to the very top.

Miriam must have refilled that jar so many times.

"You look a little sad, Bea." She didn't take any gummy bears, and neither did I.

"I'm not," I said. "I'm something, but I'm not sad."

Then I told her about how Sonia cried after she talked to her mother at night, how we listened to Grandpa's story tapes in my room (*our* room, I said), and how I wished we talked in the dark sometimes, but we didn't. We just listened to the tapes.

During the day, Sonia talked to me a lot. But when it was just us, at night, she didn't.

"Dad says that when you're homesick, nights are harder than the daytime," I told Miriam. "Dad was really homesick at camp one summer when he was a kid. Because my uncle Frank didn't go that year."

And suddenly *I* felt a little homesick, for Mom.

Dad was waiting for me outside Miriam's office, not in Mom's usual waiting-room chair, but on the other side of the room. I looked at the little table where Mom always piled her students' papers, and I told Dad I wanted to call her. He nodded and handed me his phone. Mom's number was already ringing. I sat down in her chair.

She answered, "Daniel?"

"It's me," I said.

"Hi, sweetie!"

"Hi."

"Are you at Miriam's?"

"Yeah."

"Everything good?"

"Yeah. I just wanted to say hi."

"Hi! How are things going with Sonia?"

"Good." I tried to think of something to tell her. I said, "We went to the museum. We saw the armor."

"Oh, fun! How's school going?"

"Good."

"It's good to hear your voice, honey," Mom said.

"Yeah."

Dad was holding my coat. After I said goodbye to Mom and gave him his phone back, he put my arms into my coat sleeves the way he did when I was little. It felt good. He zipped me up and tucked my hair into my hood. "Ready?" he said.

"Ready," I told him.

Sisters

That night, Sonia and I listened to my grandpa read *Harriet the Spy*.

Harriet the Spy is one of the special tapes.

We lay straight back in our beds like the girls in *Madeline*. I pressed "play."

Grandpa starts reading. But before he gets to the end of the first chapter, there's a sound. The first time I heard it, I thought it was Dad's blanket or something, brushing up against the tape recorder. But it's the sound of Dad, crying, when he was little. When Grandpa stops reading, you can really hear it.

Grandpa says, "What's wrong, Daniel?"

"I don't know." Now Dad is crying harder.

There's a pause, and I imagine Grandpa rubbing Dad's back, like Mom does for me. Then Grandpa says, "It happens sometimes. Like a passing storm."

Dad keeps crying.

"Should I read?" Grandpa says. And I can't hear an answer, but he starts up again. He reads to the end of the chapter, while Dad gets quieter. Then Grandpa says, "Better now?"

There's no answer. But I always imagine a smile from Dad.

I clicked the recorder off and waited to see what Sonia would say. We just lay there, in the mostly dark. After a minute, I sat up and looked at her.

Her eyes were open and looking straight up at the ceiling. "I miss my mom," she said.

"Yeah," I said. "That happens to me, too."

Then she pointed at the tape recorder and said, "Play."

In second grade, when I had Ms. Adams, we did an art project where we used crayons to color in every inch of a piece of paper—I did swirls, red and orange and yellow. Some kids drew rainbows. Some made squares, like a quilt.

Ms. Adams walked around, making sure we hadn't left even one bare spot of white paper anywhere. And then she handed out these extra-fat crayons, dark blue, and told us to cover up our colors, every bit of them. We rubbed and rubbed with those crayons until we laughed, because no one had told us to scribble over our work before, and also because it took so long, but then, after a while, we had done it. Every paper in the room was blue like midnight. Finally, Ms. Adams gave us wooden Popsicle sticks and told us to scratch designs into the dark, whatever we wanted. We scratched, and the colors underneath came through, surprising us.

That was how I felt that night with Sonia. Like I was waiting to find out what was underneath.

Sisters

On Sonia's last day, we went ice-skating after school. Angus came with us. The locker room was crowded and smelled like French fries, rubber, and wet socks. Sonia and Angus were both good skaters and I wasn't, but I didn't mind. Sonia showed me how to skate backward, which I could do after a while, but not fast like she did it. She said not to look over my shoulder, but I couldn't help it.

Jesse is terrible at skating. Dad took him to the middle of the ice to show him how to shift his weight, but Jesse didn't really catch on. He fell so many times that Dad made him wear both of their wool hats, one over the other, so that he wouldn't crack his head open.

After an hour and a half, Jesse said his feet hurt so much he was crying inside, so we all got off the ice to get fries at the snack window, which were a fat kind that we ate with little wooden forks. Then we went back for more skating, with Jesse sitting on a bench and waving every time we went around, like we were kids on a carousel. Finally, Dad said we should pack it in, and he yelled, "Last loop!"

I was a little bit behind everyone else, so that when I came around for my last stretch before the gate, they were all together—Dad, Jesse, Angus, and Sonia, just off the ice, waiting for me. They were waving and shouting, "Go, Bea!" like I was about to win a race.

I hunched over and sped up until I was going pretty fast—the fastest I had gone all day. I didn't slow down for the gate—I just let myself fly off the ice and hit the rubber mat, knowing they would catch me. And they did.

The locker room was still packed, and people were circling, waiting for empty lockers. I recognized a purple coat—it was Lizette's. I shouted her name, and she weaved her way over to us, with her family behind her. She was bummed we were leaving, but happy that we could give them our lockers. Jesse said he liked the green pom-poms on the toes of Lizette's skates—each pom-pom had two tiny bells hanging off it, and she shook them for us, but we couldn't hear any ringing because of all the people talking and the locker-door slamming.

I introduced Lizette to Sonia, and Lizette introduced her parents to Dad and Jesse. Lizette's mom said, "I hear you two are getting hitched," and Dad smiled this huge smile. I looked at Sonia, and she was smiling, too.

Jesse took his skates off and said, "Ahhhhh," and Sonia and I jumped up and down in our sneakers and said how they felt like pillows on our feet.

Lizette's mom told Dad, "My mom's a baker. She makes great wedding cakes. No pressure."

"Really?" Dad said. "Can you give me her number? Jesse wants this thing called a 7 Up cake that I've never even heard of."

"A 7 Up cake!" Lizette yelled. Because it turned out that 7 Up cake was one of her grandmother's favorite cakes, too.

"It's super yummy," she told me and Sonia. "Sometimes I help her, and my grandma always lets me eat the pieces that she trims off to make the cake look totally perfect before she frosts it. And sometimes I frost things, too. I'm not good enough to work on a wedding cake yet, but I can do cupcakes."

Angus had wandered over to sit on a bench next to Lizette's brother, Damian. They were both hunched over Damian's phone. I yelled "Angus!" and he looked up and waved. I had nothing to tell him. I just wanted him to see me right then.

In my head, I put the day on my list of best days.

On the bus, I felt bad that I could have a best day without Mom being in it for one minute. I watched Sonia looking out the window and realized that all of her time with us probably felt like that. Even if these weren't *best* days for her, they were days with a piece missing, like my breakfast-table diagrams. Neither one told the whole story.

Dad's phone rang as we were getting off the bus, and he answered it right away, walking ahead of us down the block. I was used to it—when Dad isn't at the restaurant, he gets a lot of calls about problems he's supposed to solve over the phone.

But when he came back, Dad told us it was Uncle Frank, and that something was wrong with my cousin Angelica.

"What happened to her?" I asked.

He said he didn't know that anything had "happened." But something was wrong with her face. The muscles on one side weren't working right.

"Does that . . . hurt?" I said.

He didn't think so. "But one side of her face is drooping, kind of. It's upsetting."

"That's awful." Jesse shook his head. "What's causing it?"

"They don't know for sure, but the doctor says it's most likely something called Bell's palsy."

"Which side of her face?" I asked.

"What?"

"Which side?"

"I didn't ask. Why?"

I was thinking about how Angelica had fallen off the loft at the lake cabin that summer. Maybe when she hit the floor, something got broken after all.

"Is there a medicine she can take for it?" I asked.

"I don't know, honey. They'll have some answers in a few days. Maybe the whole thing will be over by then." He looked at me. "Bea, you look upset. Don't be. She's going to be fine."

If she was going to be fine, why did Dad look worried?

Jesse reached out and grabbed my hand. "You're a good kid, Bea. A really good kid."

Which made me feel horrible. Really horrible.

Because I knew I wasn't good.

Sisters

Sonia stayed with us for six nights. We listened to all of *Frog and Toad*. We listened to *Harriet the Spy*. We listened to *Charlotte's Web*. We listened to *M.C. Higgins, the Great*. We stayed up very late a couple of times, even though I had school in the morning. I never fell asleep before the end of a story while Sonia was there. Dad knew we were up way past my bedtime, but he never said anything, and neither did Jesse.

Those tapes were helping. Sonia had even pushed her couch a little closer to my bed so that she could hear better. (When it got late, we turned the volume down.)

On Sonia's last night, she crouched over my tape collection, which I kept in a cardboard box in my closet.

"What about *Paddington*?" she called from inside the closet. "I used to love *Paddington*."

"Not that one," I said quickly, and she didn't ask why.

We listened to *Frog and Toad* again.

Every night, I hoped that Sonia and I would talk in the dark. It was part of the story in my head about what sisters do. But Sonia never talked. After the last *Frog and Toad* story, I clicked the tape recorder off.

"Are you tired?" I said into the dark.

She didn't answer.

We were in our nightgowns, with our beds lined up and not too far apart. Rocco was curled up on the floor, and I could hear our dads talking in the other room. Did that add up to real sisters? I didn't know.

I fell asleep.

In the morning, Jesse made waffles with butter and syrup. Sonia was happy, laughing at Dad's dumbest jokes. Nobody noticed that I barely talked, or reminded me to get ready for school. I had to remind myself.

When it was time for me to leave, they were all in the living room. Dad saw me in my coat and backpack, glanced at his watch, and jumped up. "Oops, almost time to go!"

Sonia came over and said, "I'll be gone when you get home." And again, she sounded happy.

"I won't be here, either," I told her. "I'm going to my mom's."

"Oh, right." Then she smiled.

Maybe it was just because of how much I wanted us to be real sisters, but when Sonia smiled right then, I saw something. It was like her smile said, "We know each other."

*   *   *

My mom has a funny story about when I was really little. I loved finding the moon in the sky. (The moon has always looked nice to me. Not the "pretty" kind of nice. The moon looks nice like a *person* is nice.)

My bedroom at Mom's has two windows, side by side. She says when I was little, I would point through one window and say, "Moon!" And then I would run to the *other* window, point again, and say, "*Utta* moon!"

Other moon. Because I thought that every window had its own moon.

When I said, "I'll be at my mom's," and Sonia smiled at me, I thought how my life with Mom and Dad was like a room with two big windows and two different moons. And now so was hers.

I hugged her goodbye, me in my coat, Jesse's radio playing, our sticky plates still on the table with Rocco underneath hoping it wasn't too late for something delicious to fall on the floor. When we pulled apart, Sonia's eyes were shiny. She wasn't crying, but they looked wet, maybe. When I said, "I'll miss you," and she didn't say anything back, I almost truly didn't mind.

The January Spelling Party

Dear Sonia,

How was the plane ride home? I hope no one made you eat a hot dog.

Today is the January spelling party in my classroom. Now it's just me, Carolyn Shattuck, and four other kids at our table in the lunchroom. My mom couldn't find a special dessert for my lunch, but I had the idea to put some chocolate chips in a plastic bag, so we did that. The chips are kind of old, but okay.

I think Rocco misses you. Sometimes he goes over to the orange couch and rests his head on it. He never used to do that before.

I found one of your hair bands on the rug. It's a green one. I put it in my jewelry box for when you come back.

Your future sister,

Bea

The February Spelling Party

Dear Sonia,

Carolyn Shattuck is the worst. She keeps asking me "What's on your neck?" even though I already told her it's just eczema. I'm glad you don't have it, but it would be nice to know one other person with eczema besides my uncle Frank.

My mom packed me a new word-find puzzle book, and Carolyn keeps looking over my shoulder and pointing out words. It's like she has no memory of stabbing me with that pencil in second grade.

I handed in my colonial America research paper and Mr. Home wrote "Excellent" on it and drew one of his smiley faces. He has different ones. This one had a funny hat. Sometimes I can't believe he's the same person who thinks spelling parties are a great idea.

I got your postcard (thanks!) and Jesse showed me the picture you emailed him, of you at the beach. I can't even imagine wearing a bathing suit in February! But don't worry, when you come back for the wedding it definitely won't be cold here anymore. I promise.

Your future sister,

Bea

Downright Fancy

Jesse was working behind the bar at Beatrice, setting things up for the dinner rush. Angus and I watched from our favorite bar stools, near the soda squirter. Angus had made us each a tall ginger ale, and now he was decorating them with fruit from the garnish tray.

We're only allowed to sit on the bar stools when the restaurant is closed, and we're only allowed to use the soda squirter when Jesse is there and Dad is somewhere else.

Sheila had picked us up from school and spent the whole subway ride worrying because Dad and Jesse didn't have a wedding theme yet.

"Can you believe we still don't have a theme?" She flopped back against her seat.

"Why's it so important?" Angus said.

"Because it's fun. Every fun wedding has a theme!"

"Like what?" I said.

"My cousin Anne had a beach-theme wedding. It wasn't *at* the beach, but they had sand everywhere, and people took off their shoes."

"Dad definitely wouldn't want sand in the restaurant," I said.

"No sand? Then how about Paris? The cake could look like the Eiffel Tower! No? Your face is saying no to Paris."

I laughed. "Dad will never go for a theme."

She waved at me with one hand. "Okay, maybe something low-key. Come on, *think*."

Then Angus kept saying things like "Pie wedding!" and "Candy wedding!" until Sheila looked him right in the eye and said, "You have to stop. You're blocking all of my good ideas." But the truth was none of us could think of anything good.

"It'll happen," she said after we'd been quiet for a while. "You can't force genius." She left us in front of the restaurant and clomped off in her boots.

Jesse put six oysters in front of me, just the way I like them: drowning in lemon juice.

"It wakes up your mouth!" I told Angus. But I knew Angus would never eat an oyster. "Oyster" was right after "scallop" on his nightmare list.

He held up his hand like a stop sign and said, "Too rich for my blood."

That's what Angus always says when he doesn't want to try something. I think he got that saying from his mom but doesn't realize it.

Jesse was lining up clean glasses on the shelf under the bar, and we could only see the top of his head. "Actually," he said, "oysters used to be considered low-class."

Angus reached for an olive. "How come?"

"Because oysters were everywhere, and they were cheap. But then New York City started running out of oysters. And when there weren't enough to go around anymore, rich folks got interested." Jesse stood up and stretched, bouncing on the balls of his feet. "Now they're downright fancy!"

Sometimes I forget how tall Jesse is. I held up one hand, and he slapped me five, which made me feel tall, too.

Angus shook his head. "Rich people."

"This used to be the oyster capital of the world," Jesse said. "Did you know that some of the old streets and buildings downtown were partly built with crushed oyster shells? True story. But people polluted the water and diseases got into the oyster beds, so now even if you could find one around here, it wouldn't be safe to eat it. But someday, maybe."

That's why Jesse drags all the restaurant's empty oyster shells to Brooklyn twice a week—people are trying to rebuild the New York oyster beds. He says putting a lot of old oyster shells in the water is a good way to make *new* oysters want to move in.

"Oysters actually make the water cleaner just by living there," Jesse told Angus. "They're like little vacuum cleaners."

Angus made a face. "Now I'm *never* eating one."

"Did the colonists eat oysters?" I asked Jesse.

"I'm guessing yes. Native people had been eating oysters for thousands of years before the colonists showed up. The colonists probably learned from them. It's not as if there were a bunch of supermarkets around."

Angus looked at my oysters and said, "I would have waited for a supermarket."

Jesse looked at my oysters, too. He said, "Waiting makes me hungry."

Mr. Home got super excited when I asked him whether the colonists ate oysters. It turns out Jesse was right about them learning from Native people, and that if it weren't for oysters, a lot of colonists might have starved during the winter of 1609. He said that oysters at the colonial breakfast would be "really terrific," especially if we could bring them in for free.

The final class 5-334 colonial-breakfast menu:

> *Bread* (from the store)
>
> *Handmade butter* (salt optional)
>
> *Beef jerky* (pretending it's deer meat)
>
> *Cider* (because the colonists didn't always have clean water to drink)
>
> *No chairs* (because they didn't have enough for everyone, and we didn't, either)
>
> *Free oysters* (Dad said later that he wasn't sure exactly how this happened.)

Mr. Home said table three had to get serious about our breakfast planning, now that it was March. Which meant more practice butter.

I remembered my heavy cream this time, and we brought in our clean practice-butter jars, ready to be shaken. We screwed the lids on tight and shook. And shook. And shook.

"My arm might fall off soon," Lizette said.

"I think my arm fell off already," Angus said. "Which is why I can't feel it anymore."

But I loved it. I wanted us to shake those jars together forever. When Mr. Home came over and told us we weren't even close, I was happy.

"How's Sonia?" Lizette said.

"Good," I said. I felt like I should know more things about Sonia. She was almost my sister! "She went to the beach," I said.

"Really?" Lizette rolled her eyes. "Why don't I live in California? Angus, what are you *doing*?"

"High speed!" Angus was in overdrive, shaking his jar a hundred miles an hour.

Lizette smiled. "Wanna race?"

I was about to say I didn't want to race, when there was a crash. Angus's jar had slipped out of his hands and hit the floor.

Carolyn Shattuck screamed, even though none of the mess went anywhere near her.

Mr. Home told everyone to stay away from the broken glass. The school custodian came and cleaned up while Angus apologized a lot. He looked pretty upset. Angus almost never makes mistakes.

"Share mine," I said, and Angus and I took turns shaking my jar until he looked happier and our heavy cream became a solid. I used the back of a spoon to spread some on our bread. (It wasn't French bread. It was what Dad calls plastic-bag bread.)

"Let's count," Lizette said. "One ... two ... three!"

We all took bites. It was pretty good. We had remembered salt.

"I bet they don't have bread and butter like *this* in California," Angus said, chewing.

Actually, Jesse says there's a lot of amazing food in California. But I was glad we were all in New York.

Invitations

Dad thinks an e-invite is just as good as paper, but Jesse wanted a real invitation for every guest at their wedding. He ordered them at a stationery store, and they were delivered in a heavy square box. Inside, everything fit together like a puzzle: a stack of folded invitations, a lot of big envelopes, and these little square cards that Jesse said we would put *inside* the invitations, so that people could send them back to us, saying whether or not they could come. They were called RSVP cards, and there were even little envelopes for them.

The invitation list had almost seventy people on it. (Dad said the garden at Beatrice could fit about seventy before everyone was officially squashed.) Mom and Sheila were first on the list, and Mom and Dad's college friend Melissa (mostly Mom's friend now), and Lizette and her grandmother, and Angus and (unfortunately) his parents, along with a lot of other Dad-and-Jesse friends and restaurant people. Jesse and Sheila's parents died a long time ago, just like Dad's. But our Minnesota family was coming and staying in a hotel. Dad had already made their reservation and confirmed that room service served hard-boiled eggs for Uncle Frank.

Sheila bought a calligraphy pen and addressed all the envelopes herself. Then one night after dinner we scrubbed the kitchen table, dried it carefully, and made an assembly line. It was the four of us—Dad, Jesse, me, and Sheila—and we called Sonia on Skype so that she could be there, too. Jesse made a stack of books at one end of the table and balanced his laptop on it so that Sonia's head was almost exactly as high as mine. Sonia was excited, and she even got some pieces of paper and pretended to stuff them into an envelope a few times, so it was like she was there helping us. It was pretty funny until she said, "Look, Daddy—this one's for Uncle Mission," and Jesse looked down and didn't say anything.

"Daddy!" Sonia said, still smiling. She thought he hadn't heard her. Her head was there, but her body was in California. If she'd been in the room, she would have known right away that Jesse had heard her the first time.

It was Sheila who talked finally. "Honey, you know Uncle Mission isn't coming to the wedding, right?"

"Why not?"

Sheila looked at Jesse, who was still staring at the table.

Sheila said, "Uncle Mission doesn't want to be part of your dad's life anymore."

Then Jesse talked. "Stop it, Sheel. He never said that."

I had never seen Sheila look furious before. "Jesse. He disappeared on you. How would you like me to say it?"

Jesse looked . . . afraid. I think he was afraid because Sonia was hearing what Sheila said.

"Maybe I should send him an invitation," Sonia said. "He'll come if I send it."

Sheila said, "He won't come, baby. Even if you invite him. He won't come because your daddy is marrying the man he loves, and Mission is too stupid to see that it's wonderful."

Dad had folded the invitation list into a tiny square, and he was squeezing it between two fingers. Angus told me that you can't fold a sheet of paper more than seven times. It's impossible.

Jesse was petting Rocco under the table, running his hand down the back of Rocco's head, which is what Rocco loves best. When Jesse talked, it was like he was talking to Rocco.

"I'm sorry, honey."

Sonia said, "So . . . who's gonna be there that *I* know? Besides you guys?"

"You know Angus," I told her. "And Lizette is coming. Remember her? From ice-skating?"

"I have to go," Sonia said. "It's almost dinner." And before anyone could say anything else, her hand reached out and she disappeared.

"Well, that was fun for about five minutes," Sheila said.

"Who's Uncle Mission?" I said.

Jesse said, "Mission is our brother."

"He *was*," Sheila said, slapping a "love" stamp on an envelope.

At bedtime, I asked Dad if you can get a divorce from your brother. He said no, you can't. "He's still their brother, Bea. But Sheila is angry. Mission hasn't been kind to Jesse. It's like Mission doesn't want to know Jesse anymore."

"But why?"

"Because Jesse is gay." He shook his head. "Mission doesn't know how to make room for the real Jesse. Sometimes when people want something to be one way, they just pretend."

"Does he even know about us?" Even though I hadn't known about Mission until an hour ago, this seemed rude to me.

Dad rubbed his face with one hand. "I'm guessing he knows a few things. But, Bea, this isn't about us. We're fine. We're more than fine. It isn't even about Jesse. This is Mission's problem, not ours."

"But does he know about the wedding or not?"

"I don't know, honey."

"Maybe he's waiting for an invitation. Maybe he'd come."

"I don't think he's waiting for an invitation."

"Sometimes people change," I said. "You tell me that all the time."

"You're right, Bea. Some people do change. I'm just guessing."

He said good night and started to leave. With one hand on the doorknob, he said, "Bea. Family can turn their backs on you, just like anyone else. I'm sorry to say it."

108

When Dad left, I felt awful, and I had to think through everything before I figured out why.

If Jesse's brother could turn his back on him, maybe Sonia could, too.

Maybe Sonia wouldn't choose our family, either.

Under M

My hand woke me up again that night. I closed one eye, went into the bathroom, and ran hot water over it until the itching stopped. The apartment was silent. I walked into the living room and looked at the couch—it was empty. Sheila must have gone home.

Our invitations were piled up on the table, neat stacks of them, stamped and ready. The extra invitations were still in the square cardboard box. I took one, along with an envelope and a little RSVP card.

There's a drawer in the kitchen where Dad and Jesse keep phone numbers and business cards for people like the exterminator and the farmer Dad buys chickens from. Jesse leaves his address book in there, an old black spiral. I found Mission's name under M and leaned on the kitchen counter to write his address on the envelope with the calligraphy pen. It didn't come out like the ones Sheila did, but I figured he would have nothing to compare it to.

I went back to the table. The stack of books for Sonia's head was still there, but Jesse's laptop was gone. I found the "love" stamps. Jesse had picked them especially for the wedding invitations. I stuck one on the envelope, thought about it, and put a second one on. Just in case.

I mailed the invitation the next day, on my way to school.

Walking and Talking

Miriam didn't open the door on time for our appointment that week, which had never happened before. I sat in the waiting room with Mom, listening to the hum of the noisemaker and drawing a maze all over the back cover of my math folder with a ballpoint pen. After a while, the side of my hand was all blue from ink, which matched how mad I was getting at Miriam for forgetting about me.

Finally, a woman came out, crying. She didn't look at us. She took her coat from the coat rack and left without putting it on. A wave of freezing air came in as she closed the door.

Miriam's head popped out five seconds later. "Bea, I'm so sorry I kept you waiting."

"That woman was crying," I told Miriam after we sat down. She crossed her legs. "Yes."

"So now she's just walking down the street like that? Crying?"

She waited a few seconds, and then said, "She's upset. Sometimes she cries. That's normal."

"I don't think it's normal. What happened to her? She's not even wearing her coat."

"Let's talk about you, Bea."

"I hope she stops, though," I said. "It looks so bad when you cry." I made a face, all scrunched, sticking my tongue out.

She said, "It looks so bad?"

I nodded.

Miriam didn't say anything right away. I hate it when she does that, because I know it means she wants me to think, and sometimes I'm just not in the mood.

"I have to go to the bathroom," I said. "I'll be right back." I wanted to look at my face in the mirror, to see what I was feeling, because I wasn't sure. But my face just looked like my face. For once, it wasn't saying anything.

When I came back, I said, "Sometimes I can tell my mom has been crying." It had happened two times, once in fourth grade and once at the beginning of fifth. Both times, she had come out of the bathroom pretending she had just washed her face, but I could tell.

Miriam waited.

I said, "It's like I'm not supposed to say anything. And I don't even *want* to say anything. It's like—" I stopped.

Miriam waited.

"It's almost like I feel *mad* at her."

She nodded.

"Which is really mean," I said.

She tilted her head. "Why?"

"Because it's mean to get angry at someone for *crying*."

Miriam said, "It isn't mean, Bea."

I waited. Miriam taught me to wait if you want the other person to say more.

She said, "It might be scary to think your mom has been crying."

"But then I would be scared. Not *mad*."

She waited.

I waited.

Then she said, "Remember how sometimes one feeling is behind another feeling?"

I shrugged.

She waited.

"So angry is behind afraid?" I said.

"Or maybe angry is in *front* of afraid. The angry kind of takes over."

I said, "It's like when two vowels go walking. The first one does the talking."

Miriam smiled. "You lost me."

So I explained it to her. Her face got really bright when I was talking, like she was happy. Maybe it's tiring to be the one explaining everything all the time.

* * *

biggest one), lemon cake for the middle, and chocolate cake for the top. And they are all going to have buttercream frosting. Don't worry, it tastes really good.

I wished you were there when we picked the cakes.

You accidentally turned your Skype account off, I think. I tried to send you some messages, but your light is red. When you get this, maybe you can send me an email and tell me if you turned it on again?

Your sister in seven weeks,

Bea

Bat

Something happened that April. I'm not sure it's "officially" part of the story about Dad's second wedding and the sound of corn growing, but I'm going to tell about it anyway, because everything is attached in my mind: Sonia, Angelica, Uncle Frank, the wedding, and this random bat that flew into Mom's apartment one night. (Yes, there are bats in New York City. I had never known that before, either.)

Mom shook me awake by the knees in the middle of the night. She had turned on every light in my room, and for some reason she was holding the cat.

"Don't panic," Mom said, "but we've got a bat."

I felt like my brain was still under the covers. *What?*

"Red was going nuts," she said, patting him.

The pieces were coming together. Slowly.

A *bat?*

"Where?" I sat up. I had never seen a bat up close. I jumped out of bed and went for the door, but she said, "Leave that door closed!"

"Where is it?"

Mom slid into my bed. "In the living room, last I saw. The super is coming up to get it out. He said I should open all the windows and come in here with you." She smiled. "Everything will be fine."

The doorbell rang, and Mom went out, making sure the door clicked behind her. I heard voices—hers and our super's—and then Mom came back.

"How did it get in?" I said.

"The window," Mom said. "I heard something go *bang*—it must have been the lamp hitting the floor. I went out and saw Red leaping everywhere with this terrifying face on. I haven't seen him move like that in years! At first, I thought he was after a bird. But then I saw it hang itself upside down, and I realized, oh, *bat*."

She began to look very interested in my face, scanning it. I could almost feel her eyes traveling over me, down my arms and neck, like when she was looking for eczema scratches.

"What are you doing?" I said.

"Nothing!" She was brushing my hair away from my face with her fingers, looking all along my ears, and even behind them.

"Mom! What are you *doing*?"

"I'm . . . looking for bat bites."

"*Bat bites?*"

"You were asleep, Bea. We both were. And we don't know how long that bat has been in the apartment."

I jerked away. "What are you saying? Did it *bite* us? Do bats do that? Angus told me they eat bugs!"

She pulled me back for more inspection. "I think they do eat bugs, usually. I'm sure we're fine." Then she saw the back of my neck. "Bea! Your eczema is much worse. How long have you had these scratches?"

I shrugged. "I've been itchy."

She shook her head and moved down my arms, to my hands. "You're bleeding!" She held up my hand to show me a place between my fingers. "You haven't been doing that hot-water thing, I hope. Why aren't you using your medicine?"

"Can I check *you* now?"

"What?"

"For bat bites."

"Oh—yes. I guess you should."

I lifted her hair and looked at the back of her neck, the way she had done to me. I checked her feet and ankles, and I pushed up her sleeves and stared at her arms. Everything looked normal.

"What do bat bites look like, anyway?" I said.

Mom was facing away from me, but I could see her face reflected in the dark window next to my bed. She closed her eyes.

"You know what?" she said. "I have no idea."

*   *   *

When I woke up in the morning, Red was curled around my feet. I looked at my clock and realized I was already late for school.

"Mom!"

She came in with a funny look on her face. "It's a no-work, no-school day!" she said. She plopped down on the bed and told me about how, after I'd fallen asleep, the super had finally managed to throw a towel on the bat, scoop up the bat and the towel together, and toss both out the window. The bat flew away. Mom said she wasn't opening a window for a year. Then she told me that we had to get rabies shots.

Rabies. Shots.

"But *why?*" I said. "It didn't bite us—we checked!"

She said it was impossible to rule out the possibility that it did bite one of us, because we were asleep when it came in.

"But I would know if a bat bit me!" I said. "I would have woken up!"

"Probably. But it's not worth the risk."

"Why? What happens if you get rabies?"

"There's no cure for rabies, Bea."

Oh.

"What about Red?" I asked her.

"Red gets a rabies shot every year. He's safe."

"How many shots is it?" I asked.

She didn't know.

"How big is the needle?" Dennis Mason had told me once that rabies shots are as long as a ruler and that they go straight into your stomach.

She didn't know. We were going to the doctor in an hour, and the doctor would tell us everything.

"What if it's ten shots?" I said.

She just looked at me.

"What if it's twenty-*three*?"

She laughed. "I'm pretty sure it's not twenty-three shots, Bea. And on the brighter side, Dad made us muffins and dropped them off on his way to work."

We went to the kitchen to look at them. Dad had put them in a basket I recognized from his apartment. It was strange to see that basket on the table at Mom's. And there was a note from Dad with a lot of exclamation points: "Chocolate chocolate-chip muffins!! I tripled the chocolate chips!!!"

"Triple chips?" I said, staring. There was no place on any muffin that *wasn't* covered by a chocolate chip. "For breakfast?"

She pushed the basket toward me. Which made me think that Dennis Mason was probably right about the needle.

Mom slammed a couple of glasses of milk on the table, and I managed to eat two muffins, which is how I learned I'm pretty good in an emergency. Better than I used to be, anyway.

"These are so good," Mom said.

"I know."

She swallowed and sighed. "We should really get some window screens."

Box

Dennis Mason was wrong about the bat shots. The needle is regular-size, and the shots just go in your arm like all the other ones. You don't have to get twenty-three of them. You need five, which was still five more than I wanted.

The doctor was named Dr. Thomas, and she said we only needed two shots the first day. We'd have to come back for the other ones. Mom got hers first. When it was my turn, I put on my rock face, which is what I do when I don't want anyone to know what I'm thinking. It's the face that always makes Mom ask, "What's going on in there?"

But this time she just took my hand and squeezed it.

Once, twice, three times:

I. Love. You.

I kept my rock face on but squeezed back two squeezes:

How. Much.

And waited.

Right when the doctor put the first shot in, Mom squeezed back, long and tight.

We walked home through the park, and Mom made me laugh by daring every squirrel we saw to bite her, now that she was almost rabies-proof.

At Mom's, I usually worry on my bed, cross-legged, with my back against the wall. That afternoon, I thought about Sonia, whose Skype light was still red. I thought about Jesse's brother, Mission, and whether my invitation ever got to him. I thought about Angelica. It had been a long time, but Dad said she wasn't better.

Worrying takes a lot out of me. When I opened my eyes, I was hungry.

In the kitchen, Mom was standing in front of the refrigerator, holding a big container of Dad's pasta salad. Mom and I both love it. Dad must have left us a food package while we were getting our bat shots.

"Hey," I said. "Dad came. You didn't say 'Box!'"

"Box," she said. And she reached for the salad bowl.

Late that night, full of pasta, all I could do was lie in bed and scratch. The places between my fingers and on the backs of my knees were itching like crazy. Finally, I decided to get my ointment from the bathroom cabinet. Mom had made me promise, *again*, not to use the hot-water trick.

As soon as I opened my bedroom door, I heard Mom's voice. She was on the phone.

"Of course I'm sure, Daniel. Don't be ridiculous. This has gone on too long already. No more food boxes."

—

"I'm sure. We'll be *fine*."

—

"This conversation is over. You're getting *married*, Dan—and I can certainly learn how to cook a chicken."

—

"No, I don't want you to teach me how to cook a chicken. I'll figure it out."

—

"Okay, good. And thanks again. The pasta salad was delicious. Bye."

News

I was at the kitchen table at Mom's, doing a word-find and eating tomato soup, when Dad called to say Angelica was going to the hospital.

"Oh, Daniel," Mom said. "I'm so sorry she isn't better."

"Who isn't?" I said.

Then she said, "Of course. Of *course*."

I stood up and said, "*What?*"

Mom waved at me to wait.

"Yes. She's right here. I'll tell her as soon as we hang up." And then, after a pause, "She may want some things. From your place. What time are you leaving?"

Mom hung up and told me that Angelica needed some tests. But probably she would be fine. Almost definitely.

Uncle Frank and Aunt Ess were taking Angelica to a hospital in Cleveland for a few days, and Dad was flying to Minnesota to stay with James and Jojo.

Jesse would take care of the restaurant and Rocco, Mom said. And I would stay with her until Dad came back.

I sat down. When the meaning sank in, my skin got cold.

"Dad's going to miss my colonial breakfast!" I said. Which wasn't what I meant at all.

"Bea," Mom said, "does that seem very important right now? The breakfast?"

I walked to the bathroom and threw up.

"Bea!" Mom came in and felt my forehead. "Are you sick? Why didn't you say something?"

I sat on the bathroom floor. She held a washcloth under cold water, squeezed it out, and pressed it against my cheeks. Then I let her walk me to bed.

"Honey, you should have told me you weren't feeling well. And I really am sorry about the breakfast. I wish I could cancel my trip. Do you want me to see if Melissa can go with you?"

Mom couldn't come to the colonial breakfast, either. She had a teachers' conference in Philadelphia and would be gone from early in the morning until after dinner.

"Can you talk if your face is half paralyzed?" I whispered.

"I think so," Mom said. "I'm pretty sure."

"Could it be from a fall?" I asked.

"What?"

"Angelica fell off the loft last summer. At the cabin."

"She did?"

I nodded. "Uncle Frank says her head missed the wood-stove by four inches."

"That wouldn't cause this," Mom said. "I don't think so."

127

So it was possible.

"I don't need anything from Dad's."

"What, honey?" She was rubbing my back.

"I don't need anything. Dad should go straight to the airport."

"Okay." She put the washcloth on my forehead. "You want to call him before he goes?"

I said no.

Chicken

The worst thing about getting a bat shot was all the time I spent thinking about it before I actually got it.

Mom held my hand and I stared at the wall while Dr. Thomas gave me the shot. She always had a Band-Aid ready to go, so that by the time I looked, it was already on my arm. And the shot was really no big deal, which is what I always remembered, right after.

"Do you think one side of my face looks droopy?" I asked Dr. Thomas. Mom had left the room to "do the paperwork."

"No," Dr. Thomas said, tapping on her computer, which she wheeled around with her on a rolling cart. "Why do you ask?"

"Because my cousin Angelica has a droopy half of her face now. My dad says it's this side." I slapped the left side of my face very gently. "I thought maybe it was something she caught, and maybe I caught it, too."

"I'm guessing your cousin has Bell's palsy," Dr. Thomas

said. "But it's not something you can catch. And it's temporary, almost always."

I nodded. "I know."

I guessed she thought the conversation was over, so I said, "But I just wondered. Because one time we went for a hike and we both fell down. Pretty hard. So maybe that's actually what happened."

"Fell?" She looked confused. "Beatrice, are you worried that you—rolled in something? Like poison ivy? You look fine. And your cousin—"

"Angelica," I said.

"Your cousin Angelica will be fine, I'm almost sure."

That was twice she said *almost*.

"Where did these bruises come from?" Dr. Thomas said, suddenly noticing my arm, as if it hadn't been there all along.

I'd been pinching myself hard all day, to remember what it would be like when the shot was over and done with. I'd pinch my arm and then say to myself, "See? It's over." And then do it again.

I told Dr. Thomas I didn't remember.

When we got home, Mom banged around in the cabinet under the kitchen window, asking, "Where can a roasting pan escape to?" because her friend Melissa was coming over to teach Mom how to cook a chicken. She did that until the doorbell rang.

"The roasting pan ran away!" Mom said when she answered the door. Melissa looked right past her and pointed into our living room.

"Is that it? Under your plant?"

Mom raised her arms and said, "Yes!"

I went to my room to do my worrying. I sat on the bed and closed my eyes. Mostly I worried about Angelica. And rabies. The doctor said the shots were "a hundred percent effective," but I had noticed some rabies–worry leaking in during the day. I would have worried about Sonia, but I didn't have time before the doorbell rang again.

I had invited Lizette to dinner.

"Look! Cake parts!" She held up a plastic container. "I was helping at my grandma's today. Check it out." She pulled off the top, and I saw at least three kinds of cake, cut into funny shapes.

"It's like a yummy puzzle," I said.

"Yeah, she has to trim off a lot of little pieces to make the cakes look perfect, and so I collected them. No frosting, though." She made a sad face. "Today wasn't a frosting day."

We sat on my floor with the cake between us, putting chunks of it in our mouths and trying to guess the flavors without looking, until there was only one little square left.

She did her cat smile. "Let's play halfsies. That's what I do with my brother."

"What's halfsies?"

She bit the last square of cake in half and handed it to me. "Now you bite just half of that, and then give it back."

I did. She bit *that* half in half and handed it back to me.

I laughed. "This is tiny!"

"Keep going!"

We got through three more passes, until Lizette had just a speck of cake balanced on one finger. She held it out to me. I looked at it and said, "You win, I'm not eating that!"

She licked it off her finger and said, "I always win."

I spread myself out on the floor and said, "That game is gross."

"Yeah. My mom says it's only for family. I guess you're family now."

"Thanks."

And I kind of meant it.

The chicken was good. Melissa made it, with carrots and potatoes, while Mom fiddled with the radio, made a salad, set the table, and said she was learning so much.

Lizette said the chicken was almost as good as Mom's lasagna.

Mom looked at me, and we both started laughing.

"What?" Lizette kept saying. "What?" But we wouldn't tell her.

After dinner, Mom pushed her plate away, looked at Melissa, and said, "I got Dan's wedding invitation."

"Got mine, too," Melissa said.

"We did, too!" Lizette said. She sounded way happier about it than Mom did, but Lizette didn't notice. She started telling them all about the cake her grandma was planning.

"That reminds me," Melissa said. "I brought brownies!"

Then Lizette and I looked at each other and laughed, because of all the cake we'd eaten before dinner. It was Mom's turn to say, "What's so funny? What?" But we wouldn't tell her.

We ate the brownies. And then we taught Melissa about dance-party cleanup.

When Lizette and Melissa were gone, the apartment felt really quiet. I kept trying to get Red to jump onto my bed, but he wouldn't, and I gave up.

The wedding was in five weeks.

Mission had not sent back the little card saying he would come.

I emailed Sonia before I went to bed. She didn't answer.

Messages

At school the next day, I asked Angus, "Can I come over to brush Floo-floo later?"

He looked surprised: tuna sandwich in mouth, eyebrows up. I'm not usually a big fan of going to Angus's house. But I am a fan of his cat.

"Sure," he said.

Brushing Floo-floo made me feel good. Red won't let you anywhere near him with a brush. Mom says he prefers to do his own grooming. But Floo-floo loves to be brushed—he purrs and stretches and rubs his cheeks on your sneakers. If you're holding his brush, Floo-floo will follow you anywhere.

But brushing Floo-floo meant being at Angus's apartment, which (usually) meant talking to Angus's mother.

Angus's mother had never forgiven me for pushing Angus onto the floor during musical chairs at Carrie Greenhouse's Halloween party. She also saw the exploding party bag, I think.

And I have never forgiven *her* for the third (and last) terrible party of third grade. It was Angus's birthday party, at a bowling alley uptown—the fancy one, with little menus on the seats, and people who bring your popcorn chicken and brownie bites right to your lane. I know what you are imagining, but I didn't do one thing wrong at Angus's party. I wasn't even there. Because, after Carrie's Halloween party, Angus's mother took me off the invitation list. Angus didn't know until the day after his party, when he asked me why I hadn't been there.

We lucked out for the first half hour, because Angus's mother was in her room on the phone. She works at home. She's a writer. We had four big balls of Floo-floo fur lined up on Angus's rug before she showed up in the doorway.

"Beatrice." Whenever Angus's mom sees me, she says, "Beatrice." No smile. No nickname.

"Hi," I said. "We're brushing Floo-floo."

"I see that."

"Hi, Mom."

"Hello, Angus." She didn't smile at him much, either. "And how are you two?"

"Fine," Angus mumbled.

"I'm fine, too," I told her.

"Beatrice, how is your *therapy* going? Angus says that you and your Miriam are great friends." She showed me her teeth. I think it was a smile.

Angus looked up. "I never said that, Mom."

I shrugged. "Miriam is good. We're friends, I guess. . . ."

She nodded slowly, like I was giving her a secret message that only she could understand, and said, "Well, that is wonderful."

Floo-floo stretched, reminding us that he was still available for brushing, and I got to it.

"Sorry about that," Angus said when she left. Angus gets everything. He even got why I shoved him out of that chair at Carrie's party when we were eight years old. When I apologized to him (with Carrie's mother's cold fingers on the back of my neck), he just nodded with a serious face and said, "I hate musical chairs, too."

I looked at Angus, who was making another ball of Floo-floo fur, and I remembered how hard he had been holding on to that chair.

"Angus," I said.

"Yeah?"

"You're my best friend."

"No kidding." He smiled and handed me the brush.

"Angus."

"Yeah?"

"What's it like to have a sister?" I couldn't picture Angus and his sister playing Lizette's halfsies game.

"It's good. I mean, she's old. She kind of grew up before me, you know?"

I nodded. Angus's sister is nine years older than he is. "But what does it feel like?"

He leaned back against his bed. "It's like—it's like there's someone else in my boat. Someone I don't have to explain things to."

"Because she knows?"

"Yeah. I mean, she doesn't know what it's like to *be* me, but she knows a lot of the reasons I *am* me."

"Do you think about her? Even when she's away at college?"

"Yeah. Definitely."

"I think about Sonia a lot. But I don't think she thinks about me too much."

He didn't say anything right away.

"Bea—it's not the same. I mean, you guys haven't known each other that long."

"We're not *really* going to be sisters, you mean."

He looked down. "I didn't say that."

"But that's what you *meant*."

Angus is probably the only person I never get mad at. But I was almost mad.

Jesse

While we dried dishes that night, I told Sheila about Floo-floo. "I actually used to think Floo-floo was kind of ugly," I told her. "But now that I know him, I can't believe I ever thought that. Now that I know him, he's beautiful."

Sheila gave me a long look. Then she pulled me in for a hug and said, "I love you, Bea." Sheila is like the opposite of Angus's mom.

Mom had made plans to go out because Monday is usually a Dad night, but Dad was in Minnesota. Jesse had to work at the restaurant. So Sheila had come over to Mom's to be with me.

"Can I ask you something?" I said when we were on the couch. Sheila was flipping channels.

"Always."

"How do you know for *sure* that Mission doesn't want to come to the wedding? Did you even ask him?" I was thinking that maybe I should tell Sheila about Mission's invitation. In case his RSVP card showed up in the mail.

She put down the remote and slapped her legs. "That's a big question."

I waited.

She said, "I'd have to start way back, a long time ago."

Then she stopped, and I knew she was deciding how much to say. I waited.

"Fifteen years ago, about a month before he was supposed to get married to Sonia's mom, Jesse told us he was gay. He told all of us together at the kitchen table—me, our parents, and Mission. Jesse asked us for help."

"What kind of help?"

"We all knew Ellie—that's Sonia's mom—real well, because Jesse and Ellie were high-school sweethearts. In our town, high-school sweethearts get married all the time. It's not like New York City. Ellie felt like part of the family, and now Jesse was telling us he couldn't marry her. It wasn't fair, he said, to her or to him. But he needed to know we would still be there, after. He needed . . . I think he just needed us to *say* it. That we would still be there for him, after he broke it off."

"What happened?"

Sheila closed her eyes. "You know what? I can still see us, sitting there. I'm looking at my mother's kitchen right now."

"In your mind's eye," I told her.

"Exactly." She took a deep breath. "Our mother said, 'Jesse, this never happened. We never sat here tonight, and you never said those words. Do you understand?' And then she stood up from the table. After a second, our dad got up, and then Mission stood up, too. And all three of them walked out on him. I stayed up all night with Jesse. He cried, mostly. I did, too."

"But what did she mean? When she said it never happened? I don't get it."

"It meant Jesse had to choose, Bea. He had to choose between himself and the people he loved."

It hurt, hearing that. I was pretty sure nothing like this had ever happened to Dad.

"So that's why he didn't call off the wedding? Or tell anyone else that he's gay?"

Sheila said, "I told Jesse over and over—that I loved him, and that I would be there, no matter what. I told him that we could go talk to Ellie and her family together. But it wasn't enough. *I* wasn't enough."

We heard Mom's keys in the door. Sheila leaned over and squeezed my fingers. "Some people would probably think it's wrong for me to be telling you this, Bea. But you might as well know right now that there are people who will try to make you choose between who you are and who they want you to be. You have to watch out for those people."

"Hello, gals!" Mom said. She looked happy.

"Fun night?" Sheila called to her.

"Yes!" Mom said. Her cheeks were pink and she was wearing her nice coat.

"Ooh, I love your hair pinned up like that," Sheila told her.

"But what about now?" I said quickly. "Mission might be different. Maybe we should tell him about the wedding."

Sheila stood up. "Forget about Mission, Bea." And she went to give Mom a hug.

I put my medicine on very carefully that night and tried not to scratch in bed. I laid my arms outside the covers exactly the way the doctor told me to, straight down on either side of my body. "Pretend you're a little princess," the doctor said. I remember Mom laughed.

Sheila made it sound simple, like everyone has one real self. But what if I didn't? Or what if my real self was no good? I kept imagining Angelica's face, half like usual, half not working right. Sometimes I felt like that on the inside, like I knew how I *wanted* to be, but it didn't match up with how I really was.

I closed my eyes and sent Mission a message: *Don't come.*

Definitely Maybe

Registering for a wedding sounds like something official you would do at city hall, but really it's going to a nice store and making a list of presents you hope people will give you. (Then you have to tell everyone about your list so they know exactly what you want and don't get you the wrong presents by accident.)

Dad said he didn't want to register for presents, but Jesse did, and I said I did, too, so Jesse decided we might as well do it while Dad was in Minnesota.

But first we had to drag a giant bag of oyster shells to Brooklyn.

It was a long subway ride. Jesse loves the subway. He loves it when the train comes up out of the ground, and that made me kind of love it, too, even though I had never really thought about it before. We walked to the oyster shed, Jesse dragging the bag on the ground when his arms got tired. The bag was tied at the top, but I still thought I could smell what was inside. I held my nose and walked behind him.

"You're just smelling the ocean," Jesse told me.

I made a face and pointed at the bag.

Jesse pointed back at me. "You didn't mind eating some of those oysters, though, did you?"

I do love oysters. I decided to carry the bottom of the bag so that Jesse didn't have to drag it. It was better, walking together like that. As soon as I picked it up, I felt like something was picked up inside me.

On the train back to Manhattan, Jesse surprised me.

"So what time should I be at your school on Thursday?"

"Thursday?"

"For the colonial breakfast! Isn't it this Thursday?"

"Yes, but—really? Don't you have to work?" With Dad away, Jesse was at the restaurant almost every minute.

"Don't I deserve a little time off? And who's going to open oysters for the hungry colonists?"

I hugged him. His jacket smelled like oyster shells.

At the department store, they gave us these laser pointers so that we wouldn't even have to write down the names of the presents we wanted. All we had to do was point the laser at the price tag.

At first, Jesse aimed his laser at everything in sight, saying "Maybe this? Or this?" And I said, "Definitely!" no matter what it was. He pointed at a set of solid-gold salt and pepper shakers, at a gigantic fork, and at a three-hundred-dollar cheese. I kept laughing and saying "Definitely!" and then Jesse would click his laser and add it to our list, and I would laugh harder. Then he pointed his laser at some guy's shoes, and I couldn't stop laughing. A lady walked by pushing a stroller, and Jesse pointed his laser at her purse, and then I pretended to point at the baby, and then Jesse was laughing so hard he actually sat down on the floor. If we had been two kids doing that, we would have gotten yelled at, but when you're a grown-up, I guess they leave you alone.

Eventually, we went to a computer station, where Jesse took off all the joke stuff, and we had a list of spatulas and bowls and picture frames that he liked and thought Dad would think was pretty normal, plus a waffle maker, an ice cream machine, and a two-hundred-dollar blender that Jesse said was probably a stretch, but what the heck.

Jesse said we must have done miles of walking at the store, and that we deserved some cake. We went to the department-store café, where he ordered two slices of carrot cake, which he knows I love. The slices were huge, so I cut mine in half and asked for a to-go box, for Angus. They gave it to me in a shiny pink bag with ribbon handles, and I loved holding it. The whole entire afternoon felt like a vacation from regular life. I didn't even have to remind myself not to worry.

When Jesse dropped me off at Mom's, I remembered to say thank you, and he gave me a big hug and said I was his favorite shopping partner. Then we were quiet for a second, and it was like a door opened and all my worries came zooming back: Angelica in the hospital, getting those tests. The invitation I had sent to Mission. Sonia in California, and how she still hadn't emailed me and might never come back. Jesse couldn't really be her dad from New York the same way my dad was for me. I didn't want to say it even inside my own head, but I realized that I might know Sonia's dad better than she did. It wasn't fair. I don't know what Jesse was thinking about.

Jesse

Those RSVP cards had been arriving in the mail. Almost everyone said they could come.

"The votes are in!" Sheila said. "It looks like we're having a party!" She had collected all the little cards in a shoebox, and we were sitting at the table at Dad's, eating Pizzeria Pete's and checking each name on the invitation list. There was no card from Mission. Sometimes I still wanted it to show up. Sometimes I didn't.

Mom was teaching a night class, so Sheila had picked me up from Dr. Thomas's office after our bat shots that afternoon (four down, one to go). Jesse was at the restaurant, as usual, and Dad was still in Minnesota, but it was nice to see my room at Dad's, and Rocco.

I had forgotten to do my worrying before dinner, which is probably why things kept popping up in my brain: Angelica. Sonia. Mission. I kept telling them, "I'll see you later," the way

Miriam taught me, but worries don't always listen. I took a little RSVP envelope and rubbed one sharp corner on all the itchy places between my fingers. I did it under the table, so Sheila couldn't see.

She picked up her second slice. "*Star Trek?* We're almost done with season five, I think."

"You never told me the end of the story," I said. "About Mission."

I wasn't sure she would. But she said, "Well, there isn't a whole lot more to tell. Jesse married Ellie. I had to fix his suit, though, before the wedding. He'd lost weight and it didn't fit him anymore. That's what happens when people take away their love, Bea. It makes you smaller. Sometimes it makes you disappear."

"Is that why you can't forgive Mission?" I whispered. "Because he took away his love?"

She made her eyes hold my eyes. "Yes. That's why. It was another ten years before Jesse was strong enough to tell Ellie and the rest of the world that he's gay. Our parents had died by then. And as soon as Jesse opened his mouth, Mission turned away from him again. Only, this time, Jesse was prepared. He doesn't need Mission anymore."

"But that was a long time ago, right? Maybe if someone invited Mission to the wedding, he would come."

She glanced toward the front door, as if Mission might be on the other side, or might not. "Maybe."

"Do you love Mission anymore?"

"There's something between me and Mission that can't be

broken, Bea. We were real close, all of us, growing up. We had the usual kind of adventures, I guess, but it always felt special to me."

"He's still your brother," I said.

"He's my twin."

"Twin!"

She nodded. "For a long time, Mission felt like the other half of me. But he made me choose, just like he made Jesse choose. I can't forgive him for that."

And then Sheila started crying.

I didn't know what to do. I stood up, and she opened her arms, and I sat in her lap, like I was the one who was crying.

Rocco came over and whined. He rested his chin on Sheila's knee, and we laughed. "Dumb dog," she said. And she gave him a pizza crust.

Please Don't Take

There's one part of Grandpa's tapes that was my secret for a long time. It's Dad's voice, when he was little, singing a song.

You are my sunshine, my only sunshine.
You make me happy when skies are gray.
You'll never know, dear, how much I love you.
Please don't take my sunshine away.

Grandpa isn't there. Dad must have pushed "record" again after Grandpa finished reading to him. It's a real song—I checked on the computer. He skipped some lines, but he ended up in the right place: *Please don't take my sunshine away.*

Sometimes I think about the little kid singing that song, and how he is still sort of inside Dad, all these years later.

I doubt Dad remembers. He never listens to the tapes anymore. His song is in the middle of *A Bear Called Paddington*, between chapters six and seven. That's the tape I wouldn't let Sonia listen to when she was here. I didn't want to share it, even with her.

I think Jesse is Dad's sunshine now. I'm not saying that he loves Jesse more than he loves me, or Uncle Frank, or more than he loved Mom, even. It's because Jesse is the one who might have been taken away. Jesse is who Dad wasn't sure he was allowed to have in the first place. And Jesse wasn't sure he could have Dad.

I didn't plan to tell Sheila any of this. It just happened, after she fed Rocco her last pizza crust.

She squeezed my hands, hard. "Bea. Do you know what this means? We have our wedding theme. Finally."

"We do?"

She nodded. "Sunshine."

Sheila started making a to-do list right away. "Where can we buy daisies? I want to make daisy chains. And we'll have sunflowers, sun tea . . . all nice and simple. Your dad won't mind. Oh! We can decorate the seating cards, too, a little sun on each one!" She hugged me. "Bea, I really want this wedding to be perfect. You know?"

I nodded. I did know.

By the time Mom came to pick me up, we had two pages of ideas.

"Get your stuff, hon," Mom said. "I'm starving."

"You didn't eat?" Sheila jumped up. "I want to make you something!"

"Oh no," Mom said. "I can wait."

But we made her sit down and rest on the couch while we heated up some tomato soup and Sheila made her a grilled cheese sandwich. (Grilled cheese is still the main thing Sheila likes to cook. She also likes spaghetti but says she can't stand waiting for the water to boil.)

I put out a cloth napkin and a big wineglass for Mom's water. When I led her to the table, she said, "Well, this is nice." And then we sat with her while she ate, and we all talked. Sheila and Mom can really *talk*. When it was time to go, Sheila said, "I'll walk you home with Rocco!" And we all left together.

I was about to get into bed at Mom's that night when I saw that Sonia's Skype light was green again. I called her, and she answered right away.

"Hi!" she said, like there was an exclamation point on it.

"Where *were* you? Haven't you been getting my emails?"

She made a face. "Sorry. I was kind of upset, about Uncle Mission. I didn't *know* he never talked to Daddy. Nobody told me. It was weird. It *is* weird."

I nodded. "Yeah. It is."

"Aunt Sheila called tonight. We had a pretty good talk. She talked to my mom, too. It was . . . good."

"Sheila's friends with my mom, too," I said. "That's kind of cool if you think about it. It's almost like our moms are friends."

Sonia smiled. "You never get upset, Bea. I felt so crazy when I was there, crying every night and running out of the pizza place and stuff, and you're always just—fine. Normal. Like you know what you're doing all the time."

I laughed. "I have some good stories for you. I do *not* know what I'm doing all the time." I told her about Ben Larson's speedboat party, and Carrie Greenhouse's Halloween party, and even kicking the glass with my sandal. Every story made her laugh, and it was okay because I was telling them that way on purpose.

Then she said, "Don't take this the wrong way, okay? When I was there in January, I couldn't wait to come home. I missed my mom, but it wasn't just that. I kept thinking . . . how much better I liked things before."

"Before what?"

She looked right at me. "Before I knew about you and your dad. Before Daddy started talking about me spending my vacations in New York City. It was easy before. Sometimes Daddy would come to visit me, and we'd have a really great time and everything, but that was it. Then everything would go back to normal."

I was quiet. I was afraid of whatever she was going to say next.

"But listen. After I got back here, everything felt different. I missed you guys. I missed Rocco. It was like part of me belonged in New York, with all of you. I felt like I was *missing* something, and that felt good *and* bad. Both, you know? You're used to having two places. But I'm not. I never had a home with Daddy after the divorce. But now I want to."

My happiness made me feel huge when she said that, as

big as the whole room, and I almost told her about my joy balloons, but I didn't.

I almost told her about number six on the list of Things That Will Not Change: *We are still a family, but in a different way.* But I didn't.

I almost told her about my bedroom windows at Mom's, about "utta moon," and how sometimes my life feels like a room with two windows and two moons. Then I did tell her, even though I knew she might think it was weird. Happiness makes me feel brave.

"Two moons," she said. "That's cool. It's almost like—" She stopped.

"Like what?"

"Don't laugh, but it kind of sounds like a secret power. The girls who can see two moons."

I said, "The *sisters* who can see two moons."

She grinned and made a peace sign at me. I made one back. Then a door banged open behind her and I saw one of her little brothers streak across the room in a pair of shorts and no shirt, like he had just run in from the beach or something. It's weird to turn on a computer at night in New York City and see California in the daytime.

Sonia said, "I have to go. I'm supposed to be watching my brothers."

I said, "Did Sheila tell you her idea for the wedding theme?"
"Sunshine?"

"It's great, right? But only if you like it."
She smiled. "I do."

The Colonial Breakfast

Our colonial breakfast wasn't at breakfast time—it started at 2:30, a half hour before dismissal. But Mr. Home said it was a "loose interpretation" of a colonial breakfast, anyway. A lot of colonists just stood up drinking beer in the dark for breakfast, he said, and we certainly weren't going to do that.

Jesse showed up at school right on time, waiting with his bucket of oysters in the hall with all the parents while we pushed our chairs to the walls and put out our cups of cider, our beef jerky, our bread, and our butter pots. When we were ready, Mr. Home opened the door.

Jesse filled the doorway for a second as he walked in with his big smile and his bucket. He scanned until he found me, and waved. He wore his green sweater, and he looked really nice. We all watched the play, which was called *Getting Ready for Another Day in Colonial America*. After that, everyone stood around and ate beef jerky and butter-bread for a while, and then Mr. Home played some really old songs on a violin, which he called a fiddle. I didn't even know he could do that. It was a surprise.

After we ate, Mr. Home announced that we had a special treat. The kids all sat on the rug, and the parents stood around the edges of the room. Jesse sat on a chair in front of the whiteboard with his bucket next to him and an oyster knife in one hand.

I had the job of introducing Jesse to the class, so when everyone was in their spots, I said, "The colonists ate oysters, too. New York Harbor used to be full of them. This is Jesse—he's my dad's fiancé, and he's also an oyster expert."

Then I sat down.

Carolyn Shattuck raised her hand and asked, "What's a fiancé?" and Missy told her it's like a secretary, so I stood up again and said, "A fiancé is the person you're going to marry."

Carolyn didn't wait to be called on again. "So your dad's marrying a *man*," she said.

"Yes," I said. "He's marrying *Jesse*." I pointed at Jesse.

Mr. Home said that people needed to wait to be called on before speaking.

Jesse was smiling, just waiting in the chair that Mr. Home had dragged over for him. He had his oyster-opening mitt on. "Great, let's get started," he said, and then he started talking, telling everyone about the history of oysters and New York Harbor and how the Billion Oyster Project is trying to put a billion oyster shells into the water so that, someday, oysters might decide to live in New York City again. If we're lucky.

Carolyn was whispering at her neighbors the whole time Jesse talked. Mr. Home kept glaring at her, and so did I. Then Mr. Home asked Carolyn to sit on the beanbag chair to one side of the rug. When you're sitting in the beanbag chair, you have to be silent.

Jesse ignored all of it. He opened up an oyster, washed it in the bucket of cold water, and asked the kids who wanted to try it. No one did. Suddenly I wasn't sure if no one wanted to try an oyster because it was an oyster, or because Jesse was marrying my dad.

Jesse waved the oyster around. Carolyn giggled, and I hated her.

Mr. Home said, "Carolyn." She stopped giggling.

Jesse ate the first oyster himself and said it was a demonstration. He opened another one and asked again who wanted to try. He held up the lemon slices. He had brought a little bowl of them.

I ate that second oyster, with lemon juice. Mr. Home ate the third one.

"Who else?" Jesse asked, smiling away.

No one did anything. Carolyn had a face like she was smelling something.

Lizette leaned over and whispered to me, "I'm allergic to shellfish, or I would. I swear, Bea."

Jesse just sat there looking hopeful. I could barely stand it.

That's when Angus stood up.

He walked to the front, and Jesse handed him the half shell with the oyster in it. Angus carefully squeezed a lemon slice over it. When he had it loaded up with juice, I still wasn't sure he could do it. But he ate that oyster. And then he shrugged and said, "Not as good as a brownie. But not bad."

Audrey stood up, saying she'd had oysters lots of times before. She ate one. So did Dennis Mason and a few other kids. Then Mr. Home invited the parents to join us, and those oysters were gone as fast as Jesse could open them.

I'm pretty sure the colonists didn't have lemon juice on their oysters, but Mr. Home didn't say a word.

The April Spelling Party

Dear Sonia,

Our colonial breakfast was great. The butter was good. Your dad came and opened oysters for everyone. Angus ate an oyster!

Carolyn Shattuck is sitting next to me, acting like nothing happened, but she was a jerk at the colonial breakfast. This morning when I saw her jacket in the coat closet, I took it off the hook and dropped it on the floor.

Carolyn poked me on the shoulder with two fingers. "What are you always writing?"

"Don't touch me," I said.

"Another letter, right? Who do you write the letters to?"

"I'm writing to my sister." The words gave me a happy shudder.

"You don't have a sister!" she said.

I ignored her and wrote, *I hope Carolyn Shattuck goes to a different school next year.*

"Seriously. What sister?" Carolyn had opened a bag of chips.

"When my dad gets married next month," I said slowly, "I'll have a sister. Okay?"

She laughed. "Oh, that kind of sister. Not a real one."

What a feeling feels like: When I get mad, I feel cold. I don't feel huge, like when I'm happy. It's more like I'm filling up with something that runs over my edges and rises up behind me like a gigantic pair of bat wings.

"Carolyn," I said. "Want to see a trick?"

I'd read about it in a book.

She pulled her chip bag close. "What kind of trick?"

"Hold out your hand."

"Why?" But she did it.

I held the tips of her fingers and pretended to read her palm. "I can see from these lines on your hand exactly what you had for breakfast today."

She laughed. "No way."

I could feel my bat wings uncurling above me. I stared at Carolyn's hand. "You had eggs. And ham. Ham and eggs."

She shook her head. "Wrong!"

I pretended to look confused. "You did have ham and eggs. I can see it right here." I tapped her palm. Then I leaned forward and sniffed. "Your hand even smells like ham and eggs!"

"It does not."

"Yes, it does! Smell it yourself."

My bat wings flexed.

Carolyn put her hand up to her nose to smell it.

And I bashed it into her face.

Carolyn's eyes teared up. She cupped her hands around her nose for a few seconds and then took them away, slowly.

"Do you see any blood?" She was talking to me as if I wasn't the person who had just hit her hand into her nose. In my head, I was saying "I'm sorry, I'm sorry," but on the outside, I said, "No. There's no blood. It looks okay."

"God, Bea." She wiped her eyes. "You're mean sometimes, you know that?"

The Last Bat Shot

When I got back to table three after lunch, Angus said, "What happened to you?"

"What do you mean?" I asked. "I was in the lunchroom."

He tilted his head. "You look upset."

"I'm not," I lied.

"It was a really boring spelling party," Angus said. "Mr. Home didn't even turn on the radio. I mostly read my book." He held it up, to prove it.

"Thanks," I told him.

Mom was waiting for me after school. We were going to Dr. Thomas for our last bat shots.

As soon as she saw me, she said, "What's wrong?"

"Nothing!" Sometimes I hated my face.

"Are you worried about getting the shot?"

"No."

"You're a pro now, honey. And remember, it's the last one."

"I *know*."

"How's your cousin doing?" Dr. Thomas asked me.

"My dad says she's going home from the hospital. There's no more tests to do."

"Good news."

"But she's not better. Dad says they're just 'waiting for improvement.'"

She smiled. "Life is like that sometimes."

"Dr. Thomas?"

"Yes?"

"What does rabies feel like?"

"Luckily, neither of us will ever know." She waved her shot plunger at me.

"I wonder if it feels like turning into an animal. A wild animal."

"Most animals are completely rational, Bea."

"But is it kind of like something bad in you . . . gets loose?"

"No. It's not like that. Are you still worried about having rabies, Bea?"

"Not really."

"Maybe this will help: if that bat gave you rabies, and my shots didn't work, you would already be dead. Does that make you feel better?"

It didn't.

* * *

"What were you talking about with Dr. Thomas?" Mom asked on the way home. "It seems like the minute I leave the room, you have questions. You know you can ask me questions, too, right?"

"Yeah. I know that."

"Good." She squeezed my hand. It wasn't a code. It was just a squeeze.

Before dinner, I did my worrying with my spiral notebook in my lap. I started out just doodling. Then I drew some bats. I wasn't worried about rabies anymore, but I was wondering if some kind of animal lived inside of me. I pictured Carolyn Shattuck with her hands over her nose and tears in her eyes.

I flipped to the front of my notebook and looked at the list of Things That Will Not Change. I drew an arrow that pointed from number six, *We are still a family, but in a different way*, to number twenty-three, *Jesse is staying*.

I thought about Jesse at the colonial breakfast, smiling and waiting for Carolyn's giggling to stop. I thought about Angus standing up to eat that oyster.

I wrote:

24. Jesse is brave.
25. So is Angus.

And then, underneath my bat doodles, I started writing another letter.

Dear Carolyn,

I'm really, REALLY sorry that I bashed your nose in the lunchroom. You hurt my feelings and made me angry two times this week. You laughed at Jesse during the colonial breakfast. And then today you said I would never have a real sister. That's a sore spot, because I always wanted one more than anything. I was seeing red. But I shouldn't have hurt you. I hope your nose is okay.

Also, I forgive you for stabbing me with a pencil in second grade.

Bea

On Monday, I ripped that page out of my green spiral notebook and put my letter facedown on Carolyn's chair. I felt really weird when she came in and picked it up. After she read it, she shoved my shoulder with one hand and said, "It's okay. I like your bat pictures." She didn't apologize for the things she had done. I still didn't like her. But I felt a little better anyway. About myself.

(I'm almost thirteen now, and I haven't bashed anyone, on the nose or anywhere else, since that day in the lunchroom. I think my bashing days are over.)

That night, Dad called. "I'm packing up. Angelica's home from the hospital. And guess what? She's getting better!"

"She . . . *is?*"

"The virus is going away, just like they thought it would. It took longer than usual."

"Really?"

"Really. In a couple of weeks she'll be like herself again."

"Dad?"

"Yes?"

"Will you tell her I'm sorry?"

"Sure. Why don't you make her a get-well card? She'd love that."

Mom hung up the phone for me, smiling. "Great news, right?"

It was great news. I felt good.

But I didn't feel great.

RSVP

A week before the wedding, there was a knock at Dad's door, exactly twenty minutes after we ordered from Pizzeria Pete's.

Sheila yelled, "Food!" swung her boots down from the coffee table, and jumped out of her chair. But when she opened the door, she just stood there.

"Sheel?" Jesse leaned into the living room from the kitchen. "Do you need money? My wallet is on the table."

"No," Sheila said. "But I'll take a bucket if you've got one. I think I'm going to be sick." Her hand dropped from the doorknob and she walked straight back to my bedroom, leaving the front door wide open. There was a man there, holding a green duffel bag. He had short hair and he wasn't smiling.

Jesse was coming from the kitchen. "Sheel?"

When he saw the man, he stopped.

The man hadn't moved. He was waiting, I think, to be invited inside. He said, "Hey, Jesse."

Jesse stepped forward. "Come on in, bro."

"And the man invites him in!" Sheila shouted from my room. She was walking around in there. We could hear her boots smacking the wood floor.

Jesse smiled, and the man smiled back in a way that changed his whole face. I liked his smile. He came in with his duffel bag and closed the door behind him. That was when the word *bro* sunk in. *Bro*. Like *brother*.

"Bea," Jesse said. "This is my brother, Mission. Mission, this is Bea."

"Nice to meet you, Bea." He gave me a little bow. Then he turned back to Jesse. "I'm trying to think of the right words."

Sheila's voice came sailing through again. "I have a whole lot of words! A whole lot of not-nice words!"

"Bring out your dictionary, then, Sheel!" Jesse shouted.

Mission. He was here. And Jesse was smiling.

Then the door banged open and Dad walked in with our pizza, saying, "I mugged the delivery guy in the elevator!" Which is Dad's idea of a joke, but then he saw Mission.

"This is my Daniel," Jesse said. "Dan, this is Mission. You've heard all about him."

"Of course," Dad said, smiling. Carefully.

Mission gave Dad one of his little bows and said, "May I shake your hand, sir?"

"You may," Dad said. "Let me put down this pizza first."

After he shook Dad's hand, Mission turned to me. "And may I shake your hand, Bea?" He was so formal. And I wasn't sure why Sheila had asked for a bucket. I said, "You better not. I might have rabies."

Nobody laughed.

"Bea," Dad said, "will you get us some plates?" He flipped the pizza box open on the coffee table.

"Sheila!" Jesse called. But Sheila had stopped talking, and I couldn't hear her boots on the floor anymore.

"Hungry?" Jesse asked.

Mission said, "I never say no to pizza."

Jesse laughed and said, "Well, I'm glad *some* things never change!" But then his smile fell. They looked at each other.

Dad said, "Bea. Plates, please."

Jesse, Dad, and I shared the couch, and Mission took Sheila's chair. He sat up straight and kept his feet flat on the floor, the opposite of Sheila.

Dad was mostly quiet while Jesse asked Mission friendly questions: if he wanted a Coke, if he'd taken the bus, if he was on his way to somewhere else. Mission reached into his jacket and pulled out a bent envelope, ripped open across the top. Two "love" stamps.

Dad saw the writing on the envelope, and then his eyes went right to me.

"I wanted to be here," Mission said. "For your big day."

Jesse stared at the envelope. His eyes looked full, but nothing spilled. He nodded and said, "I'm real glad you're here."

Then he turned to Dad and gave him a tight hug, like they'd just gotten good news.

Mission dropped his eyes to his plate when Jesse did that.

We left Sheila a slice of pizza, but she never came back to eat it. Dad said to give her some time alone, so I did my homework at the table while everyone watched baseball on TV. Dad spent a long time in the kitchen by himself, making popcorn.

When I went into my room for bed, Sheila was asleep on my orange couch, knees pulled up, still wearing her boots.

Dad came and checked my hand. I had been doing a better job with the ointment. Then he sat on the edge of my bed and said, "Bea." He didn't have to say anything else because I knew what he meant. He meant about sending the invitation.

"Sorry," I whispered.

Dad looked over at Sheila, and then whispered back, "*Why?*"

"I was afraid that Sonia wouldn't come back. If no one else was coming to the wedding from Jesse's family. If it was just us."

"Sonia is coming back no matter what. She's part of this family."

"Mission and Jesse are part of a family," I said.

He took a deep breath.

"He came all the way here," I said. "That's good, right? It means Jesse has a brother again."

Dad said, "I hope so."

"Dad?" I whispered. "Don't tell Sheila, okay? Don't tell her it was me."

He nodded.

"Promise?"

"Promise. Don't worry, Bea. You didn't do anything bad. Okay? This is grown-up stuff." Then he said good night and closed the door, very quietly.

In the morning, I looked at my orange couch—no Sheila. I got up and listened into the hallway, but I didn't hear Jesse's radio. I got dressed, packed my bag for school, and went into the living room.

Mission and Sheila were on the couch. He was sleeping with his head on her shoulder, and her eyes were closed. Without opening them, she said, "Is that you, Bea?"

"Yes." I held my breath.

"Don't worry, honey. It's okay."

"It is?"

"Yes, honey. Whatever happens, it's okay."

Dad came out of his room and waved me into the kitchen, where he poured us two bowls of cereal. "You said you wouldn't tell her," I whispered.

He put some pumpernickel bread in the toaster and pushed the lever down. "I didn't. She figured it out."

"Is he going to stay here?" Mission, I meant.

Dad shook his head. "He's staying at Sheila's until the wedding. Then I guess he'll go back home."

"How's Jesse?"

"He's happy," Dad said. "And sleeping late."

"So, everything is—good?"

"Yes. Everything is good." But his face looked tight.

We ate our cereal. Then I said, "Hi."

But Dad just smiled.

Box

When I let myself in at Mom's the next afternoon, there was a cardboard box on the floor under the coat hooks. On the box was a picture of an orange spoon.

"Mom?"

The toilet flushed.

"Mom?" I knocked on the bathroom door. "Did you buy a giant orange spoon?" I was thinking of the gigantic fork I saw at the department store with Jesse.

"No, silly!" she called back over the sound of running water. "That's dinner! I'm going to cook it!"

"Is Melissa coming over?"

The door opened. Mom's face looked just-washed, but not like she had been crying. "Nope," she said. "All me."

The box turned out to be full of ingredients, all just the right amount to make dinner for two: Two tomatoes. A small square of Parmesan cheese. One zucchini. Two carrots. A red pepper. Some little green peas. A skinny box of pasta. A teeny bottle of olive oil. A tiny plastic bag of salt.

And there was a shiny recipe card that said exactly what to do.

"Pasta primavera!" Mom said, waving the recipe card. "Did you know that 'primavera' means spring in Italian?" She held up the little bag of peas and smiled at it.

"Is this one of those dinner kits?" I said. "Dad always makes fun of them. He calls them 'kiddie kits.'"

Mom was reading the recipe. "I know he does. But this is great, right? They give us *exactly* what we need, and there are pictures showing *exactly* what to do. It says here to put half the salt into a pot of water." She dumped the salt onto the counter and began to divide it into two piles, pushing salt grains back and forth with a butter knife and then standing back to squint at them.

"I don't think it has to be *exactly* half the salt, Mom." I was thinking of the way Dad just threw big handfuls of salt into his pots.

"I know that," Mom said. "What am I going to do, count it? Ha!"

She followed the directions. The pasta primavera was very good.

There was no dessert in the box, so I served us each two Oreos on a square of paper towel. "Good dinner, Mom," I told her.

"It *was* good," she said, looking at my face. She wasn't looking for eczema. She was just looking at me, smiling. "It's warm in here," Mom said. "Feels like summer. Let's open some windows."

"What about the bats?" I said.

We still didn't have window screens. But we were rabies-proof now, and we decided to take our chances.

The Loft

It's funny. The whole time my cousin Angelica was sick, I never even came close to talking about what had really happened that summer. And then, suddenly, she was better, and everything was officially great: Mission had come, Jesse and Sheila were happy, Mom learned to cook something that wasn't eggs, we didn't have rabies, and Sonia was so excited about the wedding that she Skyped me almost every night. But I couldn't smile anymore. Not a real smile. And nobody noticed. I went dress shopping, and Sheila practiced doing my hair and we sent pictures to Sonia, and everyone told me how excited I must be. Part of me was excited. But part of me was really tired. I had been carrying something for a long time. I needed to put it down.

I knew where to put it. I had known that all along.

The Thursday before the wedding, when I couldn't stand it one more minute, I asked Miriam if it was possible that Angelica's face was temporarily paralyzed because she fell off the loft last summer.

"I don't know exactly which way she landed," I told Miriam, "but her head missed the woodstove by four inches."

Miriam blinked.

"Shouldn't you be writing this down?" I jabbed a finger at her notebook.

"Why, Bea? Is this important?"

I just looked at her.

She leaned forward. "We've talked about Angelica's fall. And we've talked about the fact that it's unlikely that her illness had anything to do with last summer. It was probably caused by a virus. And she's better now, right?"

"Yeah. So far."

"So far?" Miriam put her notebook down on the coffee table next to the gummy-bear jar. "Bea, do you think there's something else about last summer that we should talk about?"

"Yes," I said. Now we were both leaning forward, I noticed. We stayed like that until she said, "Bea, it looks like you're feeling sad."

I didn't say anything. I couldn't.

"Do you want to tell me what happened last summer?"

"Yes," I said. And then, for the first time ever, I cried in Miriam's office.

I Told Miriam

I pushed my cousin Angelica off the loft at our summer cabin.
Uncle Frank says her head missed the woodstove by four inches.

I Told Miriam

Every August, we opened up the lake cabin together—me, Dad, Uncle Frank and Aunt Ess, and my cousins: James, Angelica, and Jojo. There was a smell that always rushed at me when we shoved the door open: wet bathing suit plus bug spray. But it was a good smell.

The sleeping loft was just a high-up platform, barely big enough for three sleeping bags. We slept with our feet pointing toward the edge so that no one rolled off: Jojo's place was right at the top of the ladder, I was in the middle, and Angelica was against the far wall. If she came up last, she could either step over us to get to her sleeping bag or she could go along the little bit of space between our feet and the edge. That's what she was doing when I pushed her.

Everyone thinks it would be natural for me and Angelica to be close. But nothing between me and Angelica ever felt too natural.

I Told Miriam

That summer, Mom and Dad had been divorced for two years already, but Dad never invited Jesse to Minnesota. And nobody ever talked about my mom.

We were all sprawled on the tiny beach next to our dock one afternoon—me, Angelica, James, Jojo, a boy from cabin 5, and two sisters from cabin 11. We had spent the morning in the water, swamping the boats and then putting them right side up again, until we were tired. Now we were stretched out on our towels, sharing suntan lotion and gum.

James stood up and threw one of our beach balls into the water, where we watched it float past the end of our dock and head toward the middle of the lake. Usually if you threw a ball into the lake, it would float straight back to the beach, but there must have been a wind blowing the other way, because it kept moving away from us.

"You're gonna have to go get that," I told James.

"I am not," James said.

"I'll tell your dad," I said.

He ignored me. The sisters from cabin 11 had been teaching us a game where we had to clap out a rhythm and take turns singing rhymes. If someone missed a beat, they lost, and the round was over. So far, Jojo had lost twice.

One cabin 11 girl clapped and sang, "Hey, hey, my name is Joe, and my butt is bigger than Mexico."

Picking it up, Angelica clapped and sang, "Hey, hey, my name is Bill, and my butt is bigger than Hamburger Hill."

Jojo's turn. "Hey, hey, my name is Paul, and my butt is bigger than St. Paul." She was a syllable short, but everyone let it go.

Then it was my turn. "Hey, hey, my name is May—"

Without missing a beat, James shouted over the rest of my line, "AND MY BUTT'S NOT BIG, BUT MY DADDY'S GAY!"

The girls from cabin 11 laughed loud and quick, like they were getting it out of the way. I looked at them hard.

No one started a new rhyme. James didn't look at me—he got up and started chucking pebbles at the water. Angelica was watching herself wiggle her toes. She'd gotten Jojo to paint her toenails the night before. Pink.

I stood up and walked away, up the long dirt path to our porch, where Aunt Ess poured me a lemonade. Aunt Ess almost never came down to the beach. She and Uncle Frank mostly liked to sit in the big chairs facing the water, and if you stood in the wrong place, Uncle Frank would say, "You're in my sun," and that meant move.

I didn't tell on James. The truth is that my cousins love my dad especially. Dad was the only grown-up who came back from the store with kites for everyone, or a stack of Hershey bars so we could make double-stuffed s'mores. I didn't know what would happen if I told Dad what James had said, and even though I never sat down and explained it to myself, that was why I didn't tell. I didn't want anything to change.

Instead, I drank my lemonade and I scratched. Dad wasn't there to stop me. I had stupidly put on the smelly suntan lotion that the cabin 11 girls had shared at the beach. I'd wanted to slap it all over my arms and legs like Angelica and Jojo did, and say how good it smelled. Coconut.

"Itchy?"

I had forgotten that Uncle Frank was even there.

"Yeah," I said.

"I used to wear gloves to bed," he said. "Your dad ever tell you about that?"

"Yeah." Dad said that when Uncle Frank was a little kid, his eczema was so bad their mom made him wear cotton gloves at night so he wouldn't scratch.

"I hated those gloves," he said.

"Why didn't you just take them off?" I said.

"Oh, I did. Our secret. Shh." He closed his eyes.

I sat on the porch and scratched, and I watched James swim out to get that ball.

I Told Miriam

The day after I decided not to tell Dad what James said, I woke up with itchy bumps from that stupid cabin 11 suntan lotion. I had bumps on my arms and my neck and my back, and Dad said I couldn't swim or even wear my bathing suit for a whole day.

I asked Angelica if she wanted to row over to the general store, and she said nah. I asked her if she wanted to take a bike ride, and she said the girls from cabin 11 had asked her to go swimming.

They hardly swam at all, though. I could see them from our porch, where I was stuck making stretchy-band pot holders with Jojo. Angelica and the girls were lying on their towels practically all day, putting on more and more of that smelly lotion.

Then Angelica invited the girls from cabin 11 to stay for

dinner, and one of them sat in my regular chair. Dinner was bacon, lettuce, and tomato sandwiches and corn on the cob, which made me think about Natalie the pig. The summer before, I had visited Natalie in her pen behind the general store, and now she was bacon.

My stomach itched.

Aunt Ess was sitting next to me. That was another thing; I had ended up on the grown-up end of the table. Aunt Ess kept saying, "Mmm, nothing like bits and coin!" Everyone in our family calls that dinner "bits and coin" because that's what James called it when he was little. BLTs and corn is his official favorite dinner, and this was the second time in ten days that we were having it.

Seven people eating bacon, two times, plus two guests, equals sixteen servings of bacon. James basically killed Natalie.

I glared down the table at him, but he wasn't looking.

Miriam says that sometimes, when we don't want to "look hard at our behavior," we look hard at everything else instead, and that was probably why I was telling her all about bits and coin and Natalie the pig. Because what happened at dinner was that Angelica had a long, long stutter.

She got stuck on the first W:

"W-w-w-"

Her face was red from lying in the sun all day, but now she got *really* red, I think especially because those girls were there.

"W-w-w-"

Aunt Ess smiled at her and said, "Try another word, sweetie."

That's when I said, "Wh-wh-wh-what if she doesn't know any other words?"

Everyone looked at me like I had just kicked a kitten. Dad reached across, took my plate, and said, "Bea, leave the table. Now."

Angelica burst into tears.

"Burst into tears" is what people say. Usually they just mean that the person started crying. But "burst into tears" always makes me see a story in my head, like a really short cartoon: a person goes "poof" into a cloud of tears, and then the tears fall on the floor and make a puddle, and the person is gone. That's *almost* what happened with Angelica. She started crying, knocked over her water, and ran out to the porch. Aunt Ess and Jojo both ran after her.

I left the table and climbed up to my sleeping bag, feeling seasick and thinking about how I was the only kid at the table with no brother and no sister, the only one whose mother was nowhere near Minnesota. Did anyone ever think about that? And, I thought, that's *worse* than a stutter, which everyone knows you can just outgrow.

After it rains at the lake, it's really quiet. And then the birds start calling out—first it's just one bird talking, then two or three, and then suddenly they're all calling back and forth and up and down, in their different voices.

It was like that at the cabin after the horrible bits and coin dinner. First no one talked, and then Aunt Ess said something and someone answered, and then James got the Boggle game and shook it and yelled, "Who's playing?" And after that it almost sounded like normal.

I listened from the loft until Dad came up.

What a feeling feels like: When my mom is mad at me, my stomach hurts like a mouse is hitting it from the inside with a mouse-sized hammer. When my dad is mad at me, it's the same thing, except there are ten mice and ten little hammers.

It took him a long time to come. He sat on the very edge of the loft next to my sleeping bag and said, "It's dark up here. Don't you want to turn on your light?" Each of us had one of those battery lanterns near our pillows. But I shook my head. I didn't want to see his face, and I didn't want him to see mine.

He rubbed the tops of his legs and said, "Sorry I left you here so long. I was seeing red for a while."

"Seeing red" means your feelings are so worked up that you can't think straight.

"I don't care," I told Dad. "I like it up here. It's better than being down there with a lot of jerks." And then I burst into tears. Except when it was over, I was still there.

Dad put his hand on my hair. "Bea. Did something happen?"

I didn't tell him. Not about Angelica hurting my feelings all day, and not about what James said, either.

Angelica and I ignored each other in the loft that night.

The next morning, I apologized to Angelica at the breakfast table with everyone there, which Dad said I had to do. A

185

family apology, he said. At least the girls from cabin 11 weren't there. Dad and I had figured out the words together:

"Angelica, I'm very sorry for what I said at dinner last night. It was hurtful and wrong, and it won't happen again."

Dad said I should look at her when I talked, but mostly I looked at the butter. I wanted full credit, though, so at the very last second, I glanced at her. She looked mad.

"Whatever," she said.

Then Aunt Ess made her say that she accepted my apology, which I think was almost as bad for her as it was for me to say sorry in the first place, because after she accepted my apology, Angelica looked furious.

Fine. I was furious, too. Was she even thinking about the fact that I hadn't said anything about James? Or about how I felt when she didn't invite me to lie on towels yesterday? I was holding it in, and it took everything I had. It took more than I had.

After I apologized, I got busy buttering my bread, while Dad tried to convince Uncle Frank to try some bacon-and-onion omelet. Uncle Frank said he'd stick with his boiled egg. When I put the butter knife down, Aunt Ess silently pushed the sugar bowl toward me. We both like to sprinkle a little bit on top.

I Told Miriam

Mom has a saying: "And then worse met worst." That day at the lake was the worst. The girls from cabin 11 showed up right after I finished my sugar bread. We were getting our suits on. Angelica grabbed one girl with each hand, led them into her parents' bedroom, and shut the door on me. Uncle Frank and Aunt Ess were already out on the porch, in their chairs.

Friday morning was when Angelica and I always took the canoe to get Uncle Frank's newspapers at the general store. Every Friday. I waited around by the top of the porch steps for Angelica to come out. I tried to stay out of Uncle Frank's sun, and I waited, watching the door of Aunt Ess and Uncle Frank's room. My back was to the lake, which was why I almost missed seeing Angelica and the girls from cabin 11 get into our canoe and push off without me. They must have taken the deck stairs on the other side of the house, which no one did, ever. They sneaked out without me, on purpose.

I walked down to our beach and watched the canoe go around some trees and disappear. For a while, I could still hear them talking and whooping it up, and then I couldn't. I took a pointy rock and scratched my itchy arms, and then I walked into the water, but only to my ankles because I didn't have a swim buddy. I skipped about fifty rocks. On rock fifty-one-ish, James came up behind me and said, "You didn't go? I thought you love the waterslide."

And that's when I realized that Angelica and the girls from cabin 11 hadn't gone to get Uncle Frank's papers. They had gone to the waterslide.

I sat on our beach all morning, getting hotter and itchier. I went up to the house for my lunch and didn't say a word to anyone and no one even noticed. In the afternoon, I read on top of my sleeping bag in the hot loft, fell asleep by accident, and woke up feeling even worse than the worst. I climbed down and went out to the porch, where Dad and Uncle Frank were playing backgammon. I could see our canoe tied up at the dock, but Angelica had not come home.

"Who brought the canoe back?" I asked Dad. He told me that after lunch, he and Aunt Ess had driven over the bridge together, and then Ess had paddled the canoe home. The mother of the girls from cabin 11 had picked them up at the waterslide and taken them and Angelica to the arcade.

I pretended not to care.

Dad asked me if I felt like swimming.

I said, "Those girls aren't coming for dinner again, are they?"

Dad said he thought they were stopping for burgers on the way home.

That meant they were going to Burger Base.

Burger Base was on the other side of the lake, and it reminded me of Mom. (It still does.) Mom loves their onion rings. She used to say that a burger with onion rings and a Dr Pepper from Burger Base was "the perfect all-brown meal."

At bedtime, Angelica still wasn't home. Next door to Burger Base, there are go-karts, and I lay on top of my sleeping bag just knowing that she was there, driving around in circles. I loved the go-karts way more than Angelica did. She always complained about the gas smell.

By the time Angelica came back to the cabin, I was about as far from sleep as I have ever been. I felt cold. My whole body, even my skin, was listening for her. When the door finally opened, it was like a gun going off.

I heard her drop her stuff on the floor, probably a bag full of Skee-Ball prizes and candy wrappers. And then she started up the ladder.

Oyster

I cried a lot, so it took a while to tell Miriam the whole story. But finally, I finished: "She was crawling across the edge, to her sleeping bag, and she put her knee down on top of my foot, and I kind of—kicked. And she went off the side."

Miriam's expression didn't change.

"It's horrible," I told her. "*I'm* horrible. But I pretend I'm not!"

"Bea, you did something hurtful. But you are not horrible."

"What's the difference?" I cried.

"Everything you just told me makes a difference. Everything we have talked about in all the hours we've spent together makes a difference. Bea, I know you. You are not a bad person. You are a wonderful person."

"But I feel *so bad*. It's like I'm—infected."

She held up two fingers like a peace sign. "Two things. First thing: *yes*, you were angry and you hurt Angelica. Second thing: you are allowed to make mistakes. Are you hearing me? *You are allowed to make mistakes.* And to be forgiven."

Lizette had forgiven me for taking her root beer.

Angus had forgiven me for pushing him off that chair at Carrie's party.

Sheila had forgiven me for sending Mission the wedding invitation.

Even Carolyn Shattuck had forgiven me for hitting her on the nose.

"Everyone forgives me," I told Miriam.

"Everyone but *you* forgives you."

I shook my head. I couldn't talk. I finally understood why Miriam always had a box of tissues on her coffee table.

Miriam said, "There are times when it's right to be angry, Bea. And there are times when we use anger as a kind of protection from feeling hurt. It's a way of covering up."

I sniffed. "Like a pearl?"

"You lost me."

"A pearl starts with a piece of dirt that gets into the shell. The oyster slimes all over it, to cover it up. That's what a pearl is."

"Hmm."

"What?"

"Just thinking. What if the oyster didn't slime all over the dirt? What if it just let the dirt stay there and be dirt?"

"Then the dirt might hurt the oyster."

"How?"

"I don't know! I'm not an oyster!"

She laughed. "No. You are much, much better than an

oyster." Then she came over to my couch and hugged me. We were still hugging when Mom knocked on the door and poked her head in.

"Everything okay in here? It's twenty after!"

Miriam said, "Everything is great."

We never even opened the gummy bears.

That night, Red sat on my bed with me while I did my worrying. He was extra snuggly (especially for Red). I closed my eyes and tried to worry, but for once, I couldn't think of anything to worry about. Instead, in my mind's eye, I saw all these bright lines, like lasers or something, connecting me to everyone I knew. There was a line for Mom, and one for Dad, one for Sheila, one for Sonia, and one for Jesse. There were lines for Angus and Lizette and Mr. Home and Miriam and Angelica and James and Jojo and Uncle Frank and Aunt Ess and even Carolyn Shattuck and Dr. Thomas. I could see myself on the bed, with Red right next to me, and there were so many lines shooting out of me that it was like I was a flower or something, opening.

The Wedding

On the morning of Dad and Jesse's wedding, I woke up early and it was raining, hard. Sonia was on California time, so she was still asleep. But Jesse was already drinking coffee at the kitchen table with Sheila, smiling his face off.

"It's raining," I said. "You promised it wouldn't rain!"

"It's going to be a beautiful afternoon," Jesse said. "Trust me." He patted Sheila on the back. She was staring into her cup and looking miserable.

"It can't rain on your wedding, Jess," Sheila said. "It ... *can't*."

We'd all driven to the airport to pick up Sonia the night before. When Sonia and I went to bed, Sheila was at the table with her calligraphy pen, writing the words to Dad's song, "You Are My Sunshine," on squares of thick paper, one for every guest. One of Dad's high school friends was going to play his guitar while Dad and Jesse walked down the aisle, and everybody would sing the song together. Sheila had it all planned out.

Now there was a neat stack of paper squares on the table. She must have stayed up really late.

"Maybe we can do 'Singin' in the Rain' instead," I told her.

"Not funny!" She pretended to throw her toast at me.

"Where's Mission?" I said.

"At my place," Sheila said. "He's meeting us at the restaurant."

We don't call Jesse the weatherman for nothing. By three o'clock, everything was sunny and dry and felt just-washed. When we got to Beatrice, I could see myself reflected in the restaurant's front windows, and Sonia next to me. Dad had said "my guests" could come early to help, and Angus and Lizette were already standing by the door, next to a huge box.

"It's the cake!" Lizette said, pointing at the box. "We're guarding it. My grandma's parking the car."

Sonia and I decided that since we were the maids of honor, we were allowed to peek at the cake. It was three layers, beautiful and creamy-looking, and the cake smell tickled my nose.

"It actually *smells* like 7 Up!" Angus's eyes were huge, like maybe he'd just seen a unicorn. He started taking deep breaths with his head half inside the box. Lizette laughed.

"Don't breathe on it!" Sonia elbowed Angus a few steps to the side, and Lizette carefully lowered the top.

"Anyway, it's not done yet," Lizette said. "My grandma is bringing all these edible flowers to decorate it. She likes to do that part at the last minute, so they're fresh. Just wait till you see it finished."

Angus made a face and said, "I don't want flowers on my slices."

Lizette laughed. "What do you mean, *slices?*"

"Doesn't everybody get one slice from every layer?"

Lizette shoved him, and Angus pinwheeled his arms, pretending to lose his balance.

"Nobody better sit on my cake!" Lizette's grandma was jogging toward us, wearing a fancy hat and dragging a suitcase on wheels. I wondered if it was full of flowers. (It was.)

Dad unlocked the restaurant door from the inside and gave us jobs to do. First, we went around to all the tables, setting out the jugs of sunflowers Sheila had ordered. Next to the front door, we lined up little cards that told people where to sit when it was time for dinner. Sheila and I had drawn a tiny sun on each one. Then, in the garden, we opened folding chairs and lined them up in rows. Sheila showed us how to tie these big ribbons from the art store to the back of each chair, to make them look fancy. And we put one of Sheila's song cards on every seat.

Our other job was to stay out of the caterers' way. Dad said on his wedding day, someone *else* was going to cook.

It was pretty much the best afternoon of my life. In a way, I didn't want anyone else to come. Not even Mom. I wanted just me, Sonia, Sheila, Angus, Lizette, Dad, and Jesse, making everything beautiful. I stood in the garden and took a deep breath. There was a breeze, and the sun made the chair ribbons shine. Angus was making Sonia laugh—I didn't know how, and

I didn't want to know. Sheila and Lizette were dumping ice into some long coolers set up along the fence. I just stayed still and felt my happiness, the giant balloon of it.

Then Sheila said it was time for me and Sonia to get ready. We squeezed into Dad's office and got our dresses on, and Sheila pinned daisies in our hair. I couldn't believe it was all really happening, exactly the way we planned it.

When we opened the shoeboxes with our new sandals in them, I was glad Sheila hadn't let me wear mine all week the way I had wanted to. The sandals were perfect. They reminded me of a Cinderella book I used to have. I looked at Sonia, and she smiled a real smile. I knew her smiles now.

Sheila stood us side by side and held out two little white boxes.

Inside were necklaces: gold chains so thin they looked like shining thread, each with a small gold sun hanging from it. It was the most grown-up thing anyone had ever given me. Sheila did the necklace catch for Sonia, and then she did mine.

We walked out together into the dining room, where everyone was waiting for us: Angus and Lizette stood there smiling, and Dad and Jesse started clapping. If they had gotten married right then and there, it would have been a purely wonderful day.

Let's Do This

At five p.m. sharp, Sonia and I were on "door duty," welcoming people, showing them where to find their table assignments for dinner, and leading them back through the restaurant to the garden for the ceremony. I kept touching the little gold sun on my necklace, and when Angelica and her family showed up, I pretty much just held on to it.

Angelica looked just like herself. I couldn't even tell that anything had happened to her. I introduced everyone to Sonia and then walked them to the garden and gave them really good seats in the second row. I tried to say something to Angelica, but I guess I wasn't ready. I said I had to get back to the door.

"Hi, sweetie." Mom was suddenly right behind me, holding her present in both hands. She looked funny, not exactly like herself—nervous. Melissa came up next to her, smiling big enough for three people. Mom had to put the present down before we could hug, and it was like we were reaching across something to find each other. Those were the only hard seconds of the day so far. But then Aunt Ess came over and hugged Mom for a long time, and Mom's face changed. She looked like Mom. I introduced her to Sonia, and Mom hugged Sonia, too. That felt good. I decided I was ready to talk to Angelica.

She was sitting in her white folding chair, looking straight ahead while everyone stood around smiling and drinking lemonade and talking a mile a minute. I got two glasses of lemonade with two striped paper straws. I wanted to be good, but I wasn't sure if I *was* good or if I just wanted Dad and Aunt Ess and everyone to *see* me being good. Anyway, I sat down next to Angelica and gave her one of the lemonades.

I said, "So, how do you like New York?" Dad told me that they were going to spend the day "seeing the sights."

She shrugged and said, "I don't. It's kind of gross."

Dad had warned me that they probably wouldn't like it here, and he said we couldn't take it personally. "Really, Bea," he said. "Try."

So I went out of my way to say, "Yeah, it's pretty loud and crowded."

"And garbage everywhere," Angelica said, puckering her mouth. "It smells. We saw this guy? I think he was totally drunk. In the morning!"

When I looked closely at Angelica, I could see that she didn't look exactly the same as she used to. She had some zits. Sheila told me she had a million of them when she was a teenager, but now her skin looks perfect. The trick, she told me, is not to pick at them. It looked like Angelica picked hers. But I was pretty sure that if I got zits I would pick mine, too.

I took a deep breath. "Angelica," I said. "I'm sorry about last summer. It was terrible, what I did."

She smiled. "The stuttering thing? Don't worry about it." She waved at me and sucked her straw.

"Yes, that." When I thought about the bits and coin dinner, my legs felt a little seasick. "But I was actually saying sorry about—the loft."

She just looked at me.

"When you fell. I . . . *pushed* you."

Her eyebrows went up. "You did? I thought I lost my balance."

"No—your knee squashed my foot, and I kind of—" I kicked the empty chair in front of us, to demonstrate.

"Jeez, it was a two-minute thing. Did I ever show you this?" She pulled her hair back above her ear and showed me a pink mark on her scalp. "That's where James threw a piece of wood at me when he was ten. It had a nail sticking out of it! Blood *everywhere*."

"Yuck," I said.

"Yeah. Those are nice sandals," Angelica said.

"Thanks. Sonia and I got the same ones."

She nodded. "Cool."

It seemed like Angelica didn't even notice my apology. I didn't know what to do.

"Actually, I knew that you kicked me off," Angelica said.

"You did?"

"Yeah, I know the difference between falling and being pushed, Bea. Duh."

"I'm sorry."

"You said."

"I was afraid that when you fell, something happened. And that's why your face had that problem and you had to go to the hospital."

"What, because of getting my wind knocked out?"

"Yeah," I whispered.

"That wasn't why. I *know* why it happened. Karma. I got bad karma."

"You what?"

"Bad luck. I brought it on myself. I threw away a toad."

She threw away a toad?

Angelica looked at her hands again, which were just lying in her lap. Her nails looked really nice. She and Aunt Ess had probably gone for manicures.

"I was vacuuming—I have to vacuum the whole house, every Saturday. And I heard this noise in the hose that means something kind of big got sucked up. And when I looked, I saw this little toad in the canister. Ours is clear, so you can see. I don't know if it was dead or not, but I didn't—I didn't do anything. I left it there, to get dumped."

"Oh." Poor toad.

She shrugged like she didn't care, but her face looked like she was about to cry. "I don't know why I didn't let it out. I was mad about having to vacuum. There was a thing I wanted to go to with my friends, but my mom said I had to vacuum first. Anyway, the next day I woke up and my face was different. And then it got worse."

"But it might have been a coincidence about the toad," I said. "I really don't think that's why you got sick." I felt like Miriam. Maybe Angelica needed a Miriam.

She shrugged again.

"I'm sorry," I said again. I looked her right in the eyes. Not because I was supposed to, but because I wanted to. "For hurting you."

"It wasn't such a big deal, Bea. I've had the wind knocked out of me before. Relax. I forgive you."

We sat there. I did feel a little better.

"Last year stunk," Angelica said. "James was so mean all summer. Plus, my parents had been fighting a lot at home, and then at the lake they just totally stopped talking to each other, which was way worse. Everything kind of stunk."

"Your parents fight?"

She nodded. "Oh yeah. But it's a lot better now. They started counseling. We all go together sometimes. It's pretty cool, actually. You know who talks the most in counseling? James! Can you believe that? Anyway, we started having more fun, I guess, even with everyone freaking out about my face problems. This year has been a lot more fun than last year."

"Wow." It felt like Angelica and I were having our first conversation ever.

"But New York City really does smell, Bea. I mean, I can't smell it right *now*, but—P.U.! How can you live here?"

I leaned back in my chair. A daisy head pressed into my neck. "It does smell sometimes. Especially in the summer. But I like it anyway."

"So is Sonia coming to the lake this summer? And Jesse?"

"I don't know," I said. I'd never thought about that. Why couldn't they? Jesse and Dad would be married, just as much as Uncle Frank and Aunt Ess.

"Angelica," I said.

"Yeah?"

"I think you should forgive yourself. About the toad."

She stared at me.

"Okay, everyone!" Dad called out. "Let's do this!" And people cheered and started finding seats.

Vows

Dad and Jesse were getting married at the far end of the garden, where Sheila had strung a lot of paper lanterns and daisy chains along the wooden fence. The garden was mostly in the shade now, but the lights made the flowers glow a tiny bit, exactly the way Sheila said they would.

Sonia and I were in the front row, sitting between Sheila and Mom. I asked Mom to sit there with me.

"In the front row?" she said when I asked. "Won't that be— I don't know, Bea. Won't that be strange? Sitting in the front row at my ex-husband's wedding?"

But I told her strange would be if we *weren't* sitting together.

A judge was marrying Dad and Jesse. I'd been watching for a serious guy in a black robe, but he turned out to look regular, smiling in a suit. Sheila had pinned a daisy to his jacket. She had pinned daisies everywhere she could think of.

When the guitar music started, we all turned in our chairs

to look back at the restaurant door. Dad and Jesse came down the steps together, and we all started singing "You Are My Sunshine." It was even nicer than I thought it would be, hearing everyone's voices together. I looked at Sheila and she looked so, so happy. I caught her eye, and she made her smile even bigger.

Dad and Jesse walked down the aisle, just them, holding hands, all the way to the front. Then the judge started talking about how it was an honor to be there, part of a special day in our family, and how love is one of the things we should never forget to celebrate. Then Aunt Ess and Sheila each stood up to read a poem. I couldn't pay attention to the poems because I was getting really nervous. When Sheila sat down after her poem, Jesse nodded at me and Sonia, and my heart felt like thunder. It was time for the vows.

We stood up together and got next to our dads. I was squeezing Jesse's ring, and I could feel that my face was red. I looked across Dad and Jesse to Sonia on the other side, and she looked nervous, too. She waved at me and I waved back, and that made a few people laugh.

The judge said, "Jesse and Daniel have written their own vows."

That's when Mission stood up. I had forgotten all about Mission. He was near the back, in the second- or third-to-last row, but his voice was loud.

"Jesse, my man," he said.

A couple of people laughed—I guess they thought it was a joke.

Sheila stood up and faced him across all the rows of people.

Her back was to me, but I could see her face in her voice. Her voice was furious.

"Mission, what are you doing? Sit down."

Mission said, "Don't do this, bro."

Sheila had her fingers buried in her hair. "Get *out* of here, Mission. Right now."

Mission just stood there.

"*Now!*" Sheila yelled. But Mission didn't move. Nobody did.

That's when Uncle Frank and Aunt Ess started singing. They started out quiet: *You are my sunshine, my only sunshine.*

Aunt Ess has a really nice voice. On the next line, the whole second row—Angus and his parents, and Angelica, James, and Jojo—joined in. *You make me happy when skies are gray.*

Melissa and Mom were singing. Lizette and her grandmother were singing. Then it was everyone. The whole garden was singing. *You'll never know, dear, how much I love you. Please don't take my sunshine away.*

I felt frozen. But then Dad took my hand, and I saw that Jesse had Sonia's hand, and Dad had Jesse's, and the four of us were connected.

The song started again: *You are my sunshine, my only sunshine.*

Mission turned away and started to walk out of the garden, toward the restaurant, the same way Dad and Jesse had just walked in. We followed with our eyes, and the singing stayed strong.

At the steps, he turned around, and we could see his face again. We all saw the moment his eyes landed on the cake.

It was on a round table, which Sheila had covered with a tablecloth. Mission walked over to the table and stared. Lizette's grandmother had made the cake so beautiful. Tiny flowers all over it. The two tiny grooms standing on top in their suits. Sheila had even painted their ties to match what Jesse and Dad were wearing.

Dad squeezed my hand. "It's only a cake," he said. At first, I thought he was talking to me, but I realized he was talking to Jesse, whose face was like stone.

We waited. And waited. Mission was still looking at that cake and the love that had been poured all over it. And then he pushed the cake off the table. It fell on the ground. He looked at it for another couple of seconds, like he wasn't sure it was really down there.

Everyone stopped singing.

Uncle Frank stood up, fast, and walked back to where Mission was standing. I wondered if he was going to hit Mission. Dad let go of my hand and started up the aisle toward them, but Jesse said, "Daniel. Don't." And Dad stopped halfway there.

Uncle Frank didn't hit Mission. He put his face right next to Mission's and said, "It's time to go now."

I held my breath.

And then Mission ran up the steps, out of the garden, into the restaurant. From where I stood, I could see all the way through the dining room to the rectangle of sunlight that was the glass door to the sidewalk. I was afraid that Mission would start breaking things in there, but he didn't. He just kept walking away from us until he stood in the doorway—a man-shaped hole in the light that lasted a few seconds, and then disappeared.

We all looked around, and it was like waking up from a spell. The three of us—me, Jesse, and Sonia—stood together in front. Dad was still halfway down the aisle. Sonia put her arms around Jesse's middle, and he gave her a squeeze. Sheila was folded over in her seat with her head resting on her knees. Mom leaned over my empty chair to put her hand on Sheila's back. No one knew what to do next.

Uncle Frank went straight to Dad. He took Dad's hand. Holding on to it, he walked Dad back down the aisle, to us. Their feet on the gravel was the only sound. He gave Dad's hand to Jesse, who took it. Then Lizette's grandmother stood up and said, "Let's get to the important part!"

Dad said to Jesse, "What do you want to do, honey?"

Jesse said, "I want to get married, sweetie."

And they did. When the judge announced that Dad and Jesse were married, everyone—*everyone*—stood up and cheered. Sheila didn't plan that. It just happened.

Dad and Jesse hugged, then Dad and I hugged and Jesse and Sonia hugged, and then Sonia and I hugged, and I swear our sun necklaces clicked together at the exact moment that she whispered, "Sisters."

Portage

The day we walked home from school together after the colonial breakfast, Jesse told me a story. He was carrying the bucket full of empty oyster shells, swinging it.

"Bea. Did I ever tell you that I was a Boy Scout?"

"You?" I giggled.

"What's so funny?"

"Don't they wear little brown suits?"

He smiled. "They're *uniforms*."

I giggled again.

"I loved the Boy Scouts," Jesse said. "I started when I was little. When I got older, I became a trip leader. We did these wilderness trips in the summertime. I was maybe fourteen when I started doing those. We carried everything we needed, all of our food, the tents, everything, in these giant packs on our backs."

"Ugh."

"No, it was great. It was amazing. We hiked and climbed and kayaked, and every night we set up our camp and cooked our food. That food tasted unbelievable. Do you know what portage is?"

I guessed. "Mushrooms?"

He laughed. "It's when you carry your kayak over land to get to the next piece of water. We carried those boats over our heads, in teams, for *miles*. It wasn't easy.

"I led those wilderness trips for years, hiking the same trails over and over. Same woods, same hills, same stretches of river. Every trip, we lined the campers up next to the same big rock and took the same picture. But here's the thing: no two trips were the same. In fact, they were all incredibly different. You know why?"

"Why?"

"Because of the people. The other trip leaders, and the campers who came with us. They were always changing. If you think about it, Bea, life is like a trip. A very long one. And what matters most is the people you travel with."

I think it's the same with weddings. There's a lot that looks the same about them: everyone gets dressed up, says words, eats food, and gives presents. But the people at weddings are always different. And it's the people who matter. With the right people, you can carry your boat and it doesn't even feel that heavy.

Followed by Food and Dancing

The party after a wedding is called a reception. Our reception was supposed to be "food and dancing." That's what the invitations said: *Followed by food and dancing.* But for the first twenty minutes, it was more like "standing around talking and pretending to be happy." I think everyone was pretending to be *extra* happy, to make up for what had happened.

Dad was happy, he told me later. He just wasn't extra happy.

They had decided no speeches, because Jesse said speeches took time away from food and dancing. After a while, though, Dad tapped his glass with a spoon, and everyone got quiet right away, like they had been waiting for this.

Dad said, "I don't know why good days are sometimes also difficult days, but this is a good, difficult day for our family, and I'm grateful to every person here for sharing both parts of it with us. We love all of you, everyone in this room." He stopped. Then he said, "Thank you."

There was about five seconds of clapping, and then it got quiet again, like something else was supposed to happen.

I raised my hand. Dad tilted his head and said, "Bea?" It was kind of funny, I guess, me raising my hand like I thought I was in school, but no one laughed.

I said, "Can I stand on a chair? I want to say something." I don't think anyone grown knows what it's like to be short in a crowd. It's like a lot of backs.

Mom was right behind me with a chair. She held my hand while I got up on it. Suddenly I was looking at everyone's faces.

That's when I realized I didn't know what to say. I waited, like Miriam would have wanted me to. I took a minute. Inside my head, I said: *Even though Mission pushed the cake over and made everyone feel bad, especially Jesse and Sheila, I think we should celebrate, because we made a new family today. That's why we're here—to see it born. I think we should be dancing.*

What I said out loud was, "We made a new family today. I think we should be dancing."

Everyone waited. But I was done.

Then Sonia yelled, "Let's dance!" And people laughed.

Mom was still holding my hand, which I was happy about because I felt wobbly on the chair in my new sandals. And it made me feel less scared about talking. Now she squeezed my fingers—once, twice, three times. And I squeezed back—once, twice. And then she squeezed my hand really hard and reached her arms out to me. I turned and jumped, and she caught me.

Someone turned on the music, and Dad and Jesse slow-danced in a tiny space we made in the middle of all of us.

211

When the music changed, we danced. Everybody. Even Mom.

We danced for a long time. I danced with Mom, with Jesse, with Dad, and with Angus, who didn't want to dance at first, but then once he got started, danced every song. I danced with Lizette and Sonia together, and everyone made a ring around us for a minute. I didn't dance with Uncle Frank and Aunt Ess, but I saw them dancing together.

Sheila caught my hand between songs. As soon as I looked at her, she pulled me in for a hug. The next thing I knew, I was crying into her dress. "I'm sorry," I said. "I shouldn't have invited him!"

When the music started again, she swayed with me until I stopped crying. Then she held me away from her and said, "It wasn't a perfect wedding. But I don't think Jesse has ever felt more loved than he does today. That's what matters. Do you understand?"

I nodded, and she said, "Let's dance, Captain."

We ate dinner, and then we got up and danced again. Uncle Frank left the restaurant carrying his wineglass and came back with ten boxes of ice cream sandwiches. Dad and Jesse held a big knife together and cut one of them in half like it was a cake. Everyone cheered and the photographer took pictures. And then we danced some more.

What I remember is that some songs were slow and some were fast, and every time one ended, I closed my eyes and thought, "One more. Please, one more." And when the next song started, one of those joy balloons blew up inside me.

And then finally there were no more songs, and people got their purses and jackets from the coat room, but most of them didn't leave. They stood holding their things and talking, which was fine with me. Some people were helping, bringing glasses into the kitchen or dragging big garbage bags to the sidewalk. I saw Mom at the garden door, looking out into the dark. Dad walked over and they stood together, talking. I watched them until Mom felt my eyes on her back. She can do that. She turned around and waved at me to come.

I went and stood between them. We looked into the night together, and I saw it right away, even before Mom said, "Look."

The moon.

Sisters

The thing about making butter is that it feels like it'll *never* be done, almost right up to the moment when it *is* done. If what you want is butter, you have to keep going, even if you only half believe you'll get there.

It was like that with Sonia. I wanted a sister so badly, but when she first came, she wasn't my sister—she was a stranger. And all those nights she fell asleep with her back to me, it felt like she might be a stranger forever. Having a sister was like a dream that was getting further away instead of closer.

But, somehow, it had happened: we were sisters. And now she was leaving. I was one of the people who understood why she couldn't stay. Her mom was somewhere else.

In five weeks, when school was over, she would be back.

On Sonia's last night, we pushed her new bed so that it was almost touching mine, with just a crack in between. I got the tape recorder from its hiding place, and we listened to her favorite Grandpa story: *Charlotte's Web*. We listened from the beginning right through to the end, without saying one word.

The ending of that book always makes me sad, but that night it made me *really* sad. I hoped Sonia couldn't tell, but I was crying. After a minute, she got up and stood over me, her legs in that tiny space between our beds.

"Make room," she said.

I moved over, and she scooted in next to me. We talked into the darkness, making plans, until we fell asleep. And in the morning, she left.

Epilogue

Brothers

You may be asking yourself what this story has to do with the sound of corn growing. The answer isn't about corn. It's about two brothers, listening, together. It's about the kind of love that doesn't ask you to be anyone but who you are. Dad and Uncle Frank had that kind of love from the beginning. I wish everyone did.

They could never believe that other people *didn't* hear it. The most surprising thing about the sound of corn growing, Dad says, is that it's *loud*.

Acknowledgments

I want to thank a lot of people:

My unparalleled editor, Wendy Lamb, and my fantastic agent, Faye Bender, for their constant, loving, and excellent support.

My wondrous readers, Judy Blundell, Deborah Heiligman, Marthe Jocelyn, Randi Kish, Ros Kish-Levine, David Levithan, and Deborah Stead, for their questions, insights, and encouragement.

(Double-thanks to Ros for the exclamation points.)

The Random House Children's Books group, in particular the clear-eyed Dana Carey, the inexhaustible April Ward, and all the fierce and generous people who help create books and deliver them into the hands of readers, including: Tamar Schwartz, Tracy Heydweiller, Adrienne Waintraub, Lisa Nadel, Hannah Black, Colleen Fellingham, Alison Kolani, John Adamo, Joe English, Dominique Cimina, Jocelyn Lange, Judith Haut, and Barbara Marcus.

Christopher Silas Neal, for his incredible art.

Every teacher, librarian, sales rep, and bookseller who makes it the business of life to champion books for children.

My friends and family, who do so much to make the work of writing both possible and meaningful for me.